First Time Press Release Number: 5
Frist Time Press 2021 Catalog Release Number: 1
Orginal Release Date: 11/15/2021

Published by First Time Press
a protected series of S.C. TreeHouse, LLC
3928 Pattentown Rd. Ooltewah, USA, TN 37363
www.firsttimepress.sctreehouse.com

Printed in the United States of America

Soul of a Hero
Copyright © 2019 by Rob Winblad
www.storytellers.systems

Cover design: Storytellers

Published in association with Storytellers, a protected series of S.C. TreeHouse, LLC, and S.C. TreeHouse Press, a protected series of S.C. TreeHouse, LLC, and Rob Winblad.

FIRST TIME PRESS and First Time Press' logo are registered trademarks of S.C. TreeHouse, LLC.

Printed in the United States of America.
ISBN: 978-0-578-56517-0

Edited by Rob Winblad
Designed by Christopher D. Stewart

ISBN 123-45-678910-0-0

Soul of a HERO

by

ROB WINBLAD

Companion Story to
Hearts at War

First Time Press
A Storytellers Company

WELCOME

First Time
Press

Thank you for choosing to read this First Time Press book. As First Time Press we exist to give promising authors a platform to publish their early works. Since our founding, First Time Press has eagerly sought out and received submissions from authors worldwide looking for a chance to be noticed for their extraordinary creations.

What you are about to experience is raw talent. The following book has not been altered or edited by us (the publisher); instead, it is left exactly as the author wrote it. This is a showcase of an unaltered creation that we hope can inspire you to take a risk and let yourself and your work be seen.

We appreciate you taking the time to read this work of art and invite you to share in worshipping the God who has taught us all how to create.

Without further ado, we are proud to present to you the book, Soul of a Hero, and we are honored to welcome Rob Winblad back to First Time Press.

Sincerely,
Christopher D. Stewart
Founder and Owner

A fool gives full vent to his temper,
but a wise man holds it back.

- Proverbs 29:11

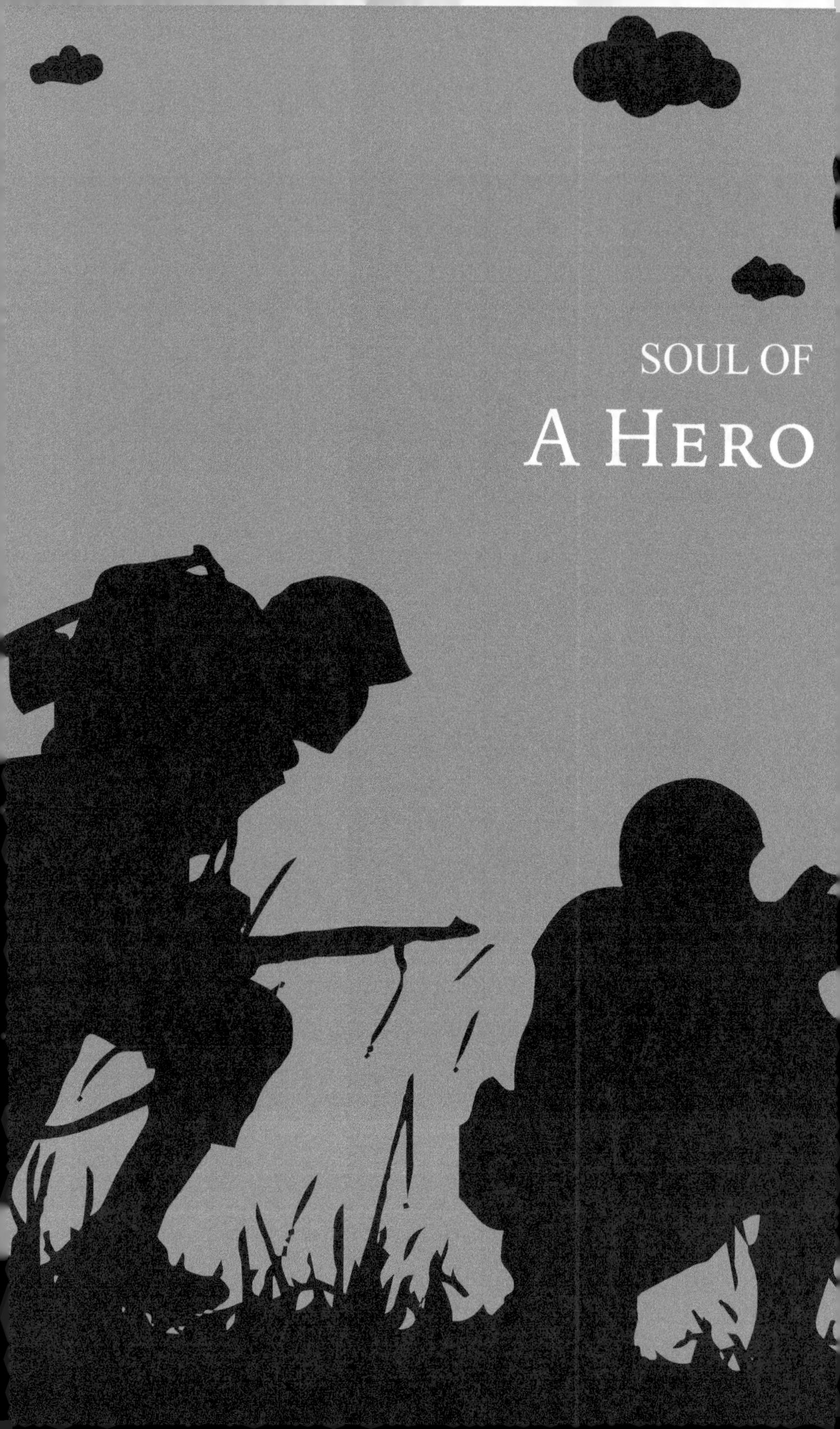

SOUL OF
A HERO

The wall of heat hit Lieutenant Carl Daniels like a hammer as he stepped off the plane. It wasn't just that it was hot; having grown up in New Mexico, he was used to temperatures that climbed up into the high nineties by nine 'o clock in the morning and liked it so much that they stayed there for the rest of the day; it was the humidity. It felt like someone had taken a giant washcloth, dipped it in warm water,

and then wrapped him up in it and stuck him in a steam bath. After taking a deep breath of the warm, soupy air, he hoisted his duffel up onto his shoulder and walked towards the staging area. His unit was technically not a separate group in and of itself, but rather replacements destined for the 503rd Infantry Regiment, 173rd Airborne Brigade Combat Team, and therefore he had been landed directly at the staging area just outside of Saigon; at Bien Hoa Air Base. According to recent reports, they had been engaged in fierce fighting, but mostly against the Viet Cong guerrillas instead of the People's Army of Vietnam regulars. Frankly, Lieutenant Daniels was just fine with that; he had signed up for a three-year tour, but once he was done with that, he was out and back home with Rhiannon; thus, if he could spend that time dueling with sub-strata peasant fighters rather than going up against full-time regulars, that was just fine by him. Climbing onto the bus with the rest of the men, he slipped shades on, staring out the window as they were driven to their barracks; a cluster of olive-drab Quonset Huts; the corrugated metal, half-round buildings that seemed to spawn from the very ground military bases were built on. Walking inside, he made for an empty bunk, unpacking and stowing his gear in the footlocker at the foot of the squeaking, reeking sleeping apparatus. Heading back outside, he learned that they had arrived just in time for dinner, and ten minutes later he was chowing down on Army-issue spaghetti and meatballs. His heart clenching as he recalled the last time he had eaten spaghetti and meatballs, he pulled out the picture of Rhiannon, cradling it in his palm as he stirred listlessly at the food. A voice above him broke into his reverie as someone jostled his shoulder. "Who's the dame, buddy?"

Turning, he looked up at the speaker, a short, pot-bellied individual with a big nose that looked as if it had been broken at least once and a Sergeant First Class's stripes on his sleeve. "My wife. Why?"

Noticing his rank insignia, the Sergeant cleared his throat, clearly re-evaluating his next words. "Um, just wanted to say, you got one fine-looking lady there, Sir. Have a nice meal, Lieutenant."

As he beat a hasty retreat, a grinning young man with short-cut sandy hair and a Lieutenant's bars plunked himself down at the table next to Lieutenant Daniels. "Don't mind Jimmy, Lieutenant. He does that to everyone who has a picture of a girl. Most of the time it's a movie star, or something like that, and he calls the guys over while he makes up conversations with her. He's really a bit of a comedian about it; he didn't mean any harm."

Nodding, Lieutenant Daniels stowed the picture back in his pocket and returned his attention to his meal. After a moment, the newcomer stuck out his hand. "I'm Mark Kentworthy. Third Platoon, Dog Company, 1st Battalion, 1/503rd."

Setting down his coffee cup, Lieutenant Daniels took the extended hand. "Carl Daniels. First Platoon, Dog Company, 1st Battalion, 1/503rd. Well, technically I'm the replacement Lieutenant for the platoon; I just got here."

Lieutenant Kentworthy brightened. "You finally got here! Great! Dog's been held on standby until our replacements got here, and it's boring as all get out."

His voice lowered as he leaned closer. "Between you and me, the last platoon commander was an idiot. He was after a high body count and glory, and his tactics showed it. That last mission, he knew they were outnumbered, but he threw his platoon into a full-on assault anyway; probably hoping for a medal and promotion for valor under fire and aggressive leadership. What he got was a half a belt of machine gun ammo that stitched him from belt to eyebrows, and two thirds of his platoon wiped out along with a quarter of Third when we went to pull the survivors out. In the end, it took an artillery barrage and three consecutive airstrikes to dislodge the position."

He trailed off, taking a slug of his coffee, then shrugged. "Ahhh, what's it matter. He's gone, and you don't seem like the kind of guy to do that stupid stuff anyway."

He lifted his cup as though to propose a toast. "To the new, smarter Lieutenant of First Platoon."

Lieutenant Daniels raised his own cup. "I'll drink to that."

The new replacements were allowed a few days to settle in, as Bravo Company was up in rotation for the search-and-destroy patrols; albeit coming toward the end of their stint. Coming off of his sentry rota halfway through the second week, Lieutenant Daniels noticed a group of soldiers clustered around a table in the recreation hall. Coming closer, he noticed SFC Lyman, the photo comedian he had met on the first day, seated across the table from Corporal Ransom; a lanky black-haired young draftee with two weeks left on his tour; a chess board sitting between them with the pieces set to mid-game. As he reached the table, Corporal Ransom, who was playing black, slid his king-side knight into position to threaten Lyman's queen-side rook. Glancing over the board, it was obvious to Lieutenant Daniels that Lyman was winning, and that Ransom's move had just created a vulnerability that would, if properly exploited, deprive him of his one remaining bishop while simultaneously creating Garde, or a direct threat to his queen. His eyebrows rising, Lyman examined the board for a moment, and then picked up his king-side bishop and moved it across the board to usurp the space formerly occupied by Ransom's bishop. "Garde."

Blanching, Corporal Ransom quickly slid his queen out of range, hesitating for a moment before settling it behind his rook. Turning to Lieutenant Kentworthy, who was also watching, Lieutenant Daniels jerked his head at the board. "Is this normal? The Chess Grand Championships playing out here in Saigon?"

One corner of his mouth twitching in a sardonic smirk at the question's mildly sarcastic phrasing, Kentworthy nodded. "Yeah. Any time he gets the chance, Lyman takes on all comers at chess. He's actually really good; I've only ever seen him beaten a few times; but he never has a shortage of challengers, and he'll take them on any time."

A loud, nasal voice broke in on the gathering as Sergeant First Class Lyman moved his knight in pursuit of the queen. "Trouncing another lamb, Lyman? You should start putting money down on these things; could make yourself quite a killing; get it, killing?"

Lips tightening, Lieutenant Kentworthy indicated the newcomer, a pale, blond-haired man with pock marks indicative of childhood acne, or possibly a bout with chicken pox, and a short flat nose parked almost carelessly between slightly sunken deep blue eyes. "With the exception of Captain Kemper. That one's just an idiot; whatever comes into his head pretty much comes out his mouth, but since he's the CO of Alpha Company, we can't really tell him exactly how we feel, so we just kind of have to put up with it."

As the men around the table began drifting away, muttering among themselves, Captain Kemper looked around in confusion. "Where's everyone going? I'm gonna break my losing streak and finally beat Lyman in the next game! Come on, guys, it's gonna be fun!"

Rolling his eyes, Lieutenant Kentworthy moved away from the table, pulling Daniels with him. "Come on; we'll come back when he's done getting his head handed to him. He's usually a pretty poor loser, and the fact that he's never won a game against Lyman so far doesn't help matters."

As they headed for the barracks, Mail Call was sounded. Accepting the envelope addressed to him, Lieutenant Daniels retired to his bunk to read the letter, which was from Rhiannon.

My dear Carl,

Although it's only been six weeks since you left, I feel as though it's been six lifetimes. I got word back from the library, and they accepted my application, so by the time you get this letter, I will be a librarian. It sounds funny to say that, thinking of you halfway across the world. Is it very dangerous where you are? I don't see much about the war on the news; it's still mostly people going on about the whole race issue. I know that we always agreed that they were justified in their fight for equality, and that the methods the government is using to suppress the demonstrations are wrong, but one of the women I was talking to at the diner said that the blacks aren't really fighting for equality, but to turn the tables on us and make us the oppressed people. What do you think?

I have to go; I can smell dinner starting to burn. I'll write to you again next week.

Love,

Rhiannon.

Folding the letter back up and sliding it back into the envelope, Lieutenant Daniels tucked it into his shirt pocket, lacing his fingers together behind his head and leaning back as he closed his eyes, allowing the last few days in New York to play on the movie screen of his mind. As the train of thought began to wind down, Rhiannon's question began to poke at his consciousness: Is it safe where I am? The first question was relatively easy to answer: Nowhere in Vietnam was ever truly safe; but there were relative degrees of safety, and Bien Hoa Airport was considered fairly safe compared to places like the Mekong Delta or the Central Highlands. As to the second question, he had no ready answer; a fact that bothered him significantly. Opening his eyes as a group of fighter jets screamed overhead on their way who knew where, he put aside the futile thoughts regarding the true agenda behind the race issue, and headed out of the barracks to see if Kemper was through with the chess game. Halfway to the recreation hall, he was intercepted by an orderly. "Lieutenant Daniels, Captain Morgan would like to see you in his office."

Exchanging salutes, Lieutenant Daniels hurried over to the Base Headquarters, wondering why the company commander wanted to talk to him. Walking into the office, he exchanged salutes with the desk Sergeant. "Lieutenant Daniels to see Captain Morgan."

Nodding, the desk Sergeant waved him through. "Go on in, Lieutenant, he's expecting you."

Opening the door to Captain Morgan's office, Lieutenant Daniels saluted. "You wanted to see me, Sir?"

Nodding, Morgan looked up from the paperwork on his desk. "Yes. At ease, Lieutenant."

As Lieutenant Daniels shifted into Parade Rest; arms linked behind his back, feet spread beyond shoulder width; Captain Morgan continued. "Dog Company is up in rotation for the patrols again, and so you and First Platoon will be going out in two days. You will be patrolling Sector Zulu, checking for Viet Cong presence as well as for sleeper agents in the villages. If you find 'em, kill 'em, but try to take at least one or two alive if you can for questioning. You will receive your full briefing package from Sergeant Winslow on your way out, and briefing your platoon at 1400 tomorrow. Any questions?"

As Lieutenant Daniels shook his head, Captain Morgan stood. "Good. Dismissed."

Exchanging salutes, Lieutenant Daniels headed back into the main office, where Sergeant Winslow handed him a file that, on closer inspection, contained a map of the sector he would be patrolling as well as the predicted mission duration and the radio callsigns for his platoon, the firebase artillery, and the A-37 Dragonfly attack aircraft and UH-1 Huey helicopters they could call on for fire support or extraction as necessary. Writing the codenames on a piece of card paper to give to the radio operator, he began working on his Mission Operational Orders, or OPORDER; the mission details he would give the men regarding mission duration, supplies they would need, and the formation they would be taking on the patrol. As he was about to begin working out the necessary supplies, Lieutenant Kentworthy poked his head in. "Hey, Carl, a couple of us got weekend passes and decided to go into Saigon to hit the bars; you want to come?"

Shaking his head, Lieutenant Daniels "Sorry, I can't come. I've still got to finish this OPORDER."

Lieutenant Kentworthy paused, clearly nonplussed. "Come again?"

Gesturing at the papers on his bunk, Lieutenant Daniels replied. "My OPORDER. My platoon is on a patrol in two days, and I'll be briefing them at 1400 tomorrow."

Lieutenant Kentworthy nodded comprehension as he turned to go. "Got it. Well, good luck."

After finishing with the OPORDER, Carl pulled out his correspondence box; a small wooden box containing paper, pencils, envelopes, and stamps that he had packed along to stay in touch with Rhiannon. Selecting a sheet of paper, he pulled out a pencil, hesitating for a moment before beginning to write:

My dear Rhiannon,

I can hardly express how happy I was to receive your letter; I'm doing well, and miss you as much as you miss me. I'm glad to hear that your application was received well; it gives me a certain peace of mind knowing that you have at least some means of supporting yourself while I'm gone. How are things at the library? It's not too dangerous where i am stationed; so far the most dangerous thing that has happened was three days ago when one of the cooks found a rat in the kitchen and chased it around with a meat cleaver screaming threats and insulting the unfortunate rodent's immediate parentage, ancestry back three or four generations, method by which it was conceived, and dietary preferences; the way he was flailing the cleaver almost scalped a couple of skivvies who got in the way when they ran in to see what was going on. That said, we are going out on patrol in a few days, so things might get a bit more dangerous. As to your acquaintance claiming that the blacks are planning to make themselves the superior ethnic group, I don't know, but I do know that the black men that I have met in the Army so far have no such visions; I cannot speak for the politically-minded among the movement, however.

Love,
Carl.

Folding the paper, he slipped it into an envelope, licked a stamp, and plastered it onto the envelope before carefully writing out Rhiannon's address and carrying it out to the Army Post Office.

The next day, he headed over to Stores with a requisition order for the extra supplies they would be needing for the mission: Claymore antipersonnel mines, rations for two and a half weeks for the platoon, ammunition, and grenades; both frag and smoke. Gathering the gear took longer than he expected, and 1400 came all too fast. He had already notified his platoon to assemble in the briefing room at the appointed time, which had tipped them off that something was happening. As the last of the men seated themselves, he indicated the map on the wall, beginning the briefing. "All right gentlemen, we are up for rotation for patrol. We will be patrolling Sector Zulu, ensuring the safety of the villagers by seeking out and destroying any and all Communist presence in our sector as well as rooting out potential sleeper agents. Rules Of Engagement are simple: Any Communist forces are to be terminated with extreme prejudice; however, if we are able to take prisoners for questioning without unduly endangering ourselves, we are to make effort to do so. The patrol should not last more than a week, and we will be able to call for artillery or air support as well as Medevac should the need arise. Intelligence suggests that there are anywhere from twenty to fifty Viet Cong in the area; but that they are likely quite spread out. One final thing. I understand that my predecessor was rather…reckless, and rumored to be in pursuit of promotion and battle decoration; and accordingly was not particularly inclined to wise battle tactics. I have no such pretensions; I've got a wife back home, who I'd like to see again, and I'd rather not rack up a body count on my own side if I can help it."

He paused to look at them for a moment, then continued. "Any questions?"

Silence greeted the query, and he nodded. "All right. We leave tonight at 1930. Pack your gear gentlemen; I've already made the necessary requisitions from Stores."

As they were leaving, the Platoon Sergeant, a tall, lean man with slightly swarthy coloring, took him aside, his deep voice tinged with a Cajun accent. "Just want to say, I's appreciate you tellin' us upfront that you not gonna just throw us into da meat grinder to get a medal."

Nodding, Carl shrugged. "Yeah; well, I figured it would help my chances of not getting in an accident if I made my position clear right off the bat."

With a slight smirk, the Platoon Sergeant followed him out to where the rest of the platoon was beginning to gather their supplies; loading and adjusting packs, selecting who was going to carry what of the munitions and extra supplies, and conversing in low tones as they speculated on what they might find out on the patrol. After dividing up the gear they would need and loading it into their packs, the platoon dispersed; most of them to get some sleep before dinner and the infiltration. 1930 came almost too soon, and then he was heading out the front gate with the thirty-odd men forming First Platoon. At the front of the column was Corporal Kit Winters, the designated point man. Short, with the high cheekbones and black hair that betrayed his Seminole heritage, he possessed an eerily good set of tracking skills that he had developed as a boy in the Florida swamps where he had grown up, hunting wild boar and deer. Next in line was Lance Corporal Tyler Masters, the burly, blond M60 gunner, followed by Private First Class Ryan Holland, the grenadier; his M79 cocked and ready. Somewhere near the middle of the column, Lieutenant Daniels trudged along with his radio operator in tow. The evening passed uneventfully, and as darkness swept over the jungle, they made camp, setting up Claymores along likely access routes toward their campsite, and opening the canned Meal, Combat, Individual, or MCI rations they had packed. With dinner over, Lieutenant Daniels set up a sentry rota and headed for his tent. Dawn was breaking as he roused the patrol, ate a hasty breakfast, and set out again, heading for the first village. As they approached the outskirts, Corporal Winters suddenly held up a fist; kneeling by the edge of the trail. Motioning Tyler and Ryan back, he gingerly parted the undergrowth to reveal the trigger attachment to a tensioned bamboo spike trap; a plate of wood with sharpened wooden stakes embedded across its' face tied to a flexible length of tree branch, which was in turn lashed to a tree trunk by a trip-line stretched across the trail. Pulling a tree branch from the side of the trail, Kit reached out and pushed hard on the trip-line, causing the spike-festooned plate to swing violently across the trail hard enough to embed the spikes in a tree on the far side. Rising to his feet, Kit nodded in satisfaction, waving the column forward. "Not bad. The big giveaway was that they forgot to put the grass back the way it was; that first tipped me off to the fact that something was out of place."

Arriving in the village, Lieutenant Daniels exchanged greetings with the headman while detailing his soldiers to check for signs of Viet Cong activity, and after receiving an 'all clear' report, began talking with the headman through a translator regarding possible evidence of Viet Cong presence in the area. There was none, and after a thorough search of the village, the patrol quickly moved out. They had three more villages to check, as well as a suspected hideout and supply cache used by the local element of VC, or Viet Cong. The rest of the day's march was boringly uneventful, and the most tension that occurred was when Sergeant Richard Powell disturbed a viper while setting up his tent. By midday of the third day, they reached the second village, with a repeat performance of the first, save that at the third village, instead of a spike trap or punji pit, Corporal Winters found a swinging punji ball trap; a criss-cross of double-ended spikes lashed together and plastered with a heavy coating of mud, which was then strung up into the trees; at the release of the trigger mechanism, the ball of spikes would swing down with tremendous force and slam into the victim's chest and face with deadly effect; even watching it pendulum harmlessly back and forth was disconcerting to the newer members of the patrol. However, like the previous villages, the patrol found no evidence of VC activity, and the headman denied any knowledge of the enemy's movements. At the fourth village, however, trouble erupted. As they were coming in, Kit uncovered two more of the swinging plate spike traps, a punji pit, and a deadly trio of Soviet anti-personnel land mines. "Okay, there's definite VC presence in the area, so watch your step," he warned as they moved forward again. On the outskirts of the village, he suddenly dived sideways behind a tree, yelling, "Ambush! Contact front! Contact front!"

Dropping to one knee behind a fallen tree that had landed slantwise against another, bigger tree, forming an almost-V, Tyler cut loose with the M60 as the distinctive 'bloop' of the M79 firing sounded to Lieutenant Daniels' right. A second later, the hut where muzzle flashes sprouted like malignant fireflies burst apart, the roof blowing off as the walls broke and collapsed under the impact of a 40mm high-explosive grenade from the M79. Popping open the breech, Holland ejected the empty cartridge, and then pulled another grenade from his web vest, sliding it into the breech before closing it and taking aim at another point of resistance. Behind them, the rest of the platoon spread out, firing bursts from their M16s as they fought to suppress the enemy fire and terminate the VC sleeper agents. Scrambling the 60mm mortar into position, the mortar team began dropping shells into the enemy huts; the thwoop of the shell firing followed a few seconds later by the crash of the two-pound shell's impact, sending flame and debris flying in all directions. Spotting a cluster of screaming civilians, Lieutenant Daniels yelled, "Watch your fire, we have noncombatants out there!"

Raising an arm or calling out in acknowledgement, several of the soldiers flipped their selectors to single-shot and began attempting to aim; but many simply tried to aim around the civilians. The very air seeming to compress around him as time slowed to a crawl, Lieutenant Daniels fought for breath, feeling as though he was being smothered; his heart hammering like the hooves of a runaway stallion, sweat pouring down his face and stinging his eyes like acid, he leveled his M16 and fired a long burst, hearing the rifle fire to his left abruptly cease as the rifle jammed. Dropping to the ground, the young man pulled the bolt back, letting it slide forward again, and then hit the forward assist before coming up firing again. A spate of bullets from one of the enemy AK-47s snapped and whined into the tree trunk above Carl's head, causing him to fall flat, a half-strangled yell ripping from his throat. Rising to his knees again, he pointed his rifle at a running VC, and pulled the trigger. Nothing happened. Gasping, he pulled the trigger again, and again, then looked down at the rifle, finally noticing the yawning gap in the side of the weapon where the bolt had locked back on an empty chamber. Kicking himself for such a rookie mistake, he dropped back to the ground, wrestling the magazine loose, fumbling a fresh magazine out of his vest, and finally fitting it into the rifle before whacking the bolt release and struggling back to his knees yet again. Peering through the smoke, he spotted a Viet Cong rifleman running out from behind the burning hut he had been using to take cover, kneeling in the middle of the street and shouldering his AK. Jerking his own weapon to his shoulder, Carl sucked in a breath, held the sights over the other man's heart, and pulled the trigger, rushing the second and third shots, but managing to keep them in the relative vicinity of his first. As if in slow motion, he watched the bullets impact, throwing the Viet Cong over onto his back, where he lay very still, blood pooling beneath him. Eyes widening, Carl hesitated for a brief instant before his head whipped around to where the M60 had fallen precipitously silent. Unhurt, but snarling his wrath, Lance Corporal Masters crouched behind cover as he struggled to change the glowing barrel without his protective mitt, which had been lost as he rushed to cover; improvising with a pad of wet leaves he had grabbed from the ground nearby, he was finding it rough going. Tugging a frag grenade loose from his vest, Sergeant Powell lobbed it in the direction of the heaviest resistance, hollering, "Frag out!"

As the grenade blew, several of the other men opened a hot fire on the enemy's left flank, and the rest of the platoon began advancing line abreast into the village, firing as they came. Suddenly the enemy was gone, with the only evidence of the combat the burning and bullet-wrecked huts, the bodies of twenty-three dead VC, six injured villagers, and three wounded soldiers of Lieutenant Daniels' platoon. Rising calmly from where he had been lying belly-down behind a tree through the duration of the firefight, Corporal Winters pulled his partially expended magazine out of his rifle, replacing it with a full one as he walked over to Lieutenant Daniels. "We should probably help these villagers, and then it's your call whether we pursue Charlie, or continue with the patrol. If you want to chase them, though, I would say move quick."

Motioning his radioman over, Lieutenant Daniels shook his head. "Nope. Not my call. But first, this is my call."

Grabbing the handset, he squeezed the talk button. "Specter One, Specter One, this is Dog One Six, do you read me, over?"

The voice of the med-evac helicopter pilot from the Casper Aviation Platoon, callsign Specter, crackled over the radio. "This is Specter, go ahead Dog One Six."

"Specter One, I have three priority casualties, requesting Dustoff, over."

"Dustoff acknowledged, Dog One Six. Specter One is inbound, twenty mikes. Specter One out."

Releasing the talk button, Lieutenant Daniels called over to the medic, who was busily attending to their wounded. "Evac is twenty mikes out."

Switching frequencies to the base headquarters, he continued. "Dog Six, Dog Six, this is Dog One Six, do you read me, over?"

Captain Morgan replied almost immediately, his disembodied voice calm and collected. "This is Dog Six, go ahead Dog One Six."

"Dog Six, I have an unknown element of Victor Charlies breaking contact. Request guidance; is pursuit advised or should we continue to next village, over?"

"Dog One Six, pursuit granted. Run them to ground, and good hunting. Dog Six out."

Acknowledging, and signing off, Lieutenant Daniels pulled his canteen out and took a long drink, then walked further into the village to check on the civilians. Two of them had been shot, and would require further medical attention at a hospital, which Daniels relayed on to Crop Duster; the others had relatively minor shrapnel wounds, and one had a broken leg where a falling hut beam had landed on her. Patching them up and treating the gunshot victims as best as he could, Sergeant Powell helped the others check for evidence of 'stay-behinds', or guerrillas who might have remained in the area to cover the retreat of the main force. Letting his mind wander as he awaited the report, Lieutenant Daniels found himself reliving the firefight, and he flinched as his mind's eye replayed the killing of the Viet Cong guerrilla; the look on the man's face as he fell, his eyes wide in pained shock; the hands clutching at his chest as blood spurted from the wounds. Suddenly a hand on his shoulder jerked him out of his reverie, and he looked up at Kit, who had walked up while he was lost in thought. "You okay, Sir?"

Nodding shakily, Lieutenant Daniels waved a hand. "Yeah, sure; it's just…" he trailed off, unsure how to explain. The corner of Kit's mouth quirked understandingly. "First time in combat, Sir?"

Averting his eyes in embarrassment, Lieutenant Daniels nodded again. "Yeah."

Corporal Winters squatted down so that he could look Lieutenant Daniels in the eye again. "Look, Sir, that's nothing to be ashamed of. The first time I was in combat, I screamed like a little girl in a haunted house. I was scared out of my mind; but I can also say that it gets easier with repetition. Killing's the same way; the first time you actually see the guy go down will probably stay with you for a long time, but you learn not to think about it. Besides, most of the time you'll never see it happen. I'll bet you killed a couple of those guys out there in the village, but it wasn't obvious. That's the way most of the people you kill out here will be; you'll never see 'em, so don't worry; and don't think about it."

As he rose to his feet, Lieutenant Daniels grabbed his hand in a firm handshake. "Thank you, Corporal."

Corporal Winters shrugged, a millimetric smile on his face. "Don't mention it, Sir. I got the same talk after my first firefight, so I figured the least I could do was pass it on. So what's the word on pursuit?"

Nodding, Carl pushed to his feet with a grunt. It was

startling how tired he was after the engagement; despite the relatively short length of the engagement, adrenaline had drained him badly enough that he felt as though he had just run five miles. "Granted. 'Run them to ground, and good hunting', as Captain Morgan put it."

Nodding, Corporal Winters went to inform the rest of the patrol. Walking over to where Tyler was reassembling his M60 after clearing a jam. "So how long do you have left?"

Clearly misunderstanding the query, which was intended to determine how much time he had left in-country, Lance Corporal Masters hastily slapped the feed cover down on the breech. "Just finished Sir. We going after them?"

Lieutenant Daniels shook his head. "Yes, but what I meant was, how long do you have left in-country? You know, how long until your tour is over?"

Lance Corporal Masters gave a grunt of comprehension as he began putting his cleaning kit back in the bag. "Oh. To answer the second question, I've got about two months left, but to answer your second question, however long this blasted war is going to take. You see, Sir, I volunteered, and I'm going to keep re-upping."

Lieutenant Daniels looked incredulous. "What? Why in the holy blazes would you do that? I took a three-year tour, sure, but when that's done, that's it; I'm out of here; no offense."

Lance Corporal Masters shrugged. "None taken. The reason is, I love my country, and, well, the Army's been my family for as long as I can remember. I'm an Army brat, see. I grew up on Army bases, enlisted when I was seventeen, and I'm probably going to stay on until they retire me. I'm a lifer, Sir; plain and simple."

He seemed about to continue, when the sudden, distinctive whup-whup-whup of chopper rotors clattered in the distance, growing louder by the second, and he checked his ramblings to run back into the brush with an exclamation of annoyance. Looking after him in bewilderment, Lieutenant Daniels looked at Private First Class Holland. "What's with him?"

Looking over the items the big Lance Corporal had left in his wake, Private First Class Holland shrugged. "My best guess is he decided now would be a good time to go find his mitt, though what prompted him to remember to look for it now is beyond me. But then again, a lot of what he does is beyond me."

His prediction proved correct, as after thrashing about in the brush for a moment or two, Lance Corporal Masters returned in triumph, busily knotting a spare shoelace around a loop in the mitt, and tying the other end of the second shoelace to his load-bearing harness. "Now let's see it get lost!"

As he checked to make sure that he had enough space to actually use the mitt with it tied to his harness, giving a grunt of approval before tucking it back into its proper pouch, Sergeant Powell shook his head disapprovingly. "Famous last words, Lance Corporal. Famous last words."

Further conversation was cut off as the choppers circled once before descending on the Landing Zone, or LZ, that had been marked by a green smoke grenade. Jumping out as the first UH-1 settled on its skids, a team of medical evacuation personnel came racing over, bent almost double in the churning rotor wash. The next few minutes were a hectic blur of activity as the medics quickly stabilized the casualties, strapped them on stretchers, and rushed them to the waiting helicopters; the patrol 'standing to' in a defensive perimeter around the Landing Zone to ensure protection against any marauding Viet Cong. None materialized, and the Hueys lifted off amidst a flurry of dust and grass as the rotors pitch and rate increased to raise them above the trees, their racket fading away over the horizon as they headed back to the airbase. Turning to the rest of the platoon, Lieutenant Daniels re-slung his pack, motioning for them to do likewise. "Okay, men, let's move out."

Platoon Sergeant Roland Bellamy's deep voice boomed as he echoed Carl's command. "Y'all heard de Lieutenant! Move it out!"

Re-gathering, the platoon headed down the trail at a pace that tried to combine caution and speed, following the trail the Viet Cong had left. Clearly they had either not expected pursuit, or didn't care, as they were leaving a trail that was not unduly difficult to follow. The next four days were spent in hot pursuit, with the enemy always just one step ahead of them. As the pursuit continued, it soon became evident that they were heading for the Vietnam/Cambodian border; undoubtedly seeking sanctuary across the border. On the afternoon of the fifth day, with no real change in the paradigm of the pursuit, Lieutenant Daniels radioed headquarters. "Dog Six, this is Dog One Six. I have yet to regain contact with the element of Victor Charlies; suspect they are heading for Cambodia. Request permission to break pursuit and continue sector patrol, over."

Captain Morgan's voice was sympathetic, but firm, as he replied. "Permission denied, Dog One Six. Maintain pursuit; keep pushing them. Dog Six out."

Signing off, Lieutenant Daniels gently slammed the handset back into its holding cradle as his frustration leaked out into his actions. As he clenched his teeth, counting to thirty in an attempt to get back in control of his emotions, Corporal Winters walked over. "What's the verdict?"

Lieutenant Daniels held up one finger in a 'wait-a-minute' gesture, and finished counting before turning to face Corporal Winters. "Sorry, what did you say?"

Corporal Winters raised one eyebrow, but nonetheless repeated himself. "I said, what's the verdict, Sir?"

Lieutenant Daniels nodded. "Oh. Sorry. We keep pushing them."

As Corporal Winters was about to turn away, he continued. "I wasn't trying to remind you to say 'Sir', I was taking a second to get my temper back under control, and I didn't really hear what you said."

Turning back, Corporal Winters looked at him with new respect in his eyes. "That a fact, Sir?"

As Lieutenant Daniels nodded, he gave an approving grin. "Now that's something I imagine a lot of officers could do with learning."

Lieutenant Daniels shrugged. "Yeah; it's somewhere in the Bible about that; something about only a fool lets his temper go, or something like that. I didn't want to be a fool growing up, so I decided to learn how to keep a lid on my temper, and on what I was thinking. As I recall, the verse said something like, 'his spirit', referring to what the fool lets go, and I couldn't for the life of me figure out whether that meant your temper or your thoughts, so I clamped a lid on both."

Shrugging again, he changed the subject. "Anyway, the request to continue the patrol has been denied, so we keep chasing these guys."

Walking up in time to hear the last sentence, Private First Class Holland snorted. "What I'd like to know is, why are we being ordered to chase them, even though it should be obvious to even a complete idiot; not saying that Captain Morgan is one, you understand; that they're going to just slip across the border into Cambodia, and that's the last we'll see of them until they're good and ready for us to see them again?"

Lieutenant Daniels shrugged. "I don't know. I just don't know.

Corporal Winters looked speculative, but remained silent. Noticing his expression, Lieutenant Daniels spoke.

"Spit it out, Corporal. What's on your mind?"

Corporal Winters hesitated for a moment, then nodded. "It's just a thought; something I heard about a couple of months back. It could be that we're pushing these guys toward a Hatchet Team or Ma Rung."

Lieutenant Daniels and Private First Class Holland looked at each other, then at Corporal Winters, bemused expressions on their faces. Lieutenant Daniels was the first one to speak. "Hatchet Team? Ma Rung? What on Earth are you talking about?"

"Well, Hatchet Teams are a special forces group that are part of a sort of secret branch of MACV which operates in this area, as well as up near the DMZ and behind enemy lines. They're mostly a reconnaissance group, but they also will capture enemy personnel, or occasionally kill them, as well as sometimes raiding and sabotaging the Ho Chi Minh trail. And Ma Rung is a Vietnamese word meaning 'Jungle Ghosts'; it's an epithet for the Navy SEALs."

His voice grew grave as he continued. "If there are SEALs around here, then Hell itself is loose in these jungles."

The little group was silent for a moment, then Lieutenant Daniels cleared his throat. "Well, we'd best get moving again. Who knows, the Cong may have slowed down enough that we can catch them."

Amid sardonic laughter and cynical snorts at the thought of how likely that was going to be, they headed back to where the rest of the group was having lunch. "All right, we're continuing pursuit, so let's move out!"

With stifled groans, along with several muttered remarks about the stupidity of their pursuit, the platoon resumed the march, eyes alert for booby traps or ambushes laid by the fleeing Cong. As night fell, they made a hasty camp; not bothering with tents, the men simply rolled up in their ponchos and blankets as the sentries alternately paced and knelt behind trees, eyes straining to pierce the darkness. Rising with the dawn, they continued to move, finding evidence of their enemy's passage, but no enemies. As the sun was going down, however, they suddenly heard a series of sharp explosions, followed by a blaze of gunfire ahead of them. Snapping to sharp attentiveness, Corporal Winters broke into a jog. "That can't be more than a mile or so ahead of us! Let's move!"

Trying to run through the jungle undergrowth while still keeping an eye out for traps, the platoon listened tensely as the sound of firing reached a crescendo, and then faded to a few scattered pops and snaps, then died away completely. Slowing down, they approached the area with growing caution, unsure of who won, or even who exactly had been engaged. Finally they arrived on the scene of the battle. Scattered around in the brush and bamboo stands were the bodies of some twenty or thirty Viet Cong, some obviously hit by Claymore Mines or blown apart by explosives, others gunned down where they stood. Surveying the scene carefully, Kit began reconstructing it, musing aloud as he moved from one angle to another. "Hmm. Okay, looks like at least two, possibly three Claymores went off, probably by command; hard to tell… wait, nope, at least one of them went off by tripwire; here's the trigger assembly. From the shell casings, it looks like there was a machine gun here…riflemen here, here, and here…they didn't move around much; just sat and fired mostly. Over here, the VC weren't expecting a fight, so they probably just panicked and started spraying bullets, but the Claymores weren't in front of the riflemen, they were in the main line of predicted travel, while the riflemen were over on the flank. Looks like at least one or two of the ambushers got hit, probably not too badly."

"How can you tell?" Inquired Lieutenant Daniels. Turning from his inspection of a broad-leafed plant, Kit looked confused. "Which part?"

Lieutenant Daniels shrugged. "Everything, I guess."

"Yeah; all I can see is that a bunch of gooks got whacked," added Private First Class Holland.

Stifling a sigh, Kit explained. "Well, as to the Claymores, these bushes here are shredded in a pattern that tallies with the shrapnel pattern of a Claymore; as well as burn marks on these tree trunks that suggests the back-blast of a Claymore; I can't tell if it was two, or three with two close together because of the way these marks are. The riflemen's position, as well as the machine gun, I can tell because of shell casings over here. The shell casings in this pile are all M60 cartridges, and the shell casings scattered over here are all M16 cartridges. The enemy fire I can roughly deduce from the damage to the trees and brush higher up than the Claymore would have done, as well as which side of the tree is being hit; an ambusher who missed would have damaged this side of the tree, but as you can see, the damage is on the other side of the tree, so it had to have been one of the VC."

Private First Class Holland interrupted. "How do you know it wasn't a rifleman from the ambush party on the other side of the ambush?"

Kit walked over to the area indicated. "Well, it could be, but there are no cartridge casings in the area."

As Private First Class Holland shut up, Kit walked back over to the area that the ambushers had been firing from. "And lastly, as to my conjecture that the ambush party had at least two members injured, but not badly, these bloodstains on the leaves here. They are in two distinctly different places, so it's obviously two different people, but there's not a huge, huge amount of it; just some splatter on the branches here, so they're probably not suffering from big, bleeding holes in their bodies, just little leaking ones to make them complain and need some bandaging."

Lieutenant Daniels gave a smirk at Kit's choice of words, then motioned to his Communications Sergeant.

Pulling the handset free, he spoke. "Dog Six, Dog Six, this is Dog One Six, do you read me, over?"

"Dog One Six, this is Dog Six, go ahead."

"Dog Six, I have regained contact with the Victor Charlie force; but they've been terminated. My point man believes it was an ambush; possibly by MACV personnel, or else Navy SEALs."

Captain Morgan was silent for a moment, then spoke. "Good work, Dog One Six, resume patrol of the villages."

Lieutenant Daniels breathed a silent sigh of relief. "Roger that, Dog Six, Dog One Six out."

Turning to the rest of the platoon, he gave a grin. "All right, men, we're back on track for the patrol. Let's move out!"

Within a few minutes, they were heading for the last village in the sector; this one the furthest out, as well as the closest to the Vietnam/Cambodian border. This close to the Ho Chi Minh Trail, Viet Cong and NVA presence was statistically likely to be stronger, and the firebase artillery had been notified to be on standby for the duration of their stay in the vicinity of the border. Lieutenant Daniels had wanted to have A-37 Dragonflies overhead on Close Air Support standby, but had been informed that the low flight endurance of the aircraft did not permit it. Arriving at the village without incident, they found no booby traps whatsoever in the area surrounding the village. While Lieutenant Daniels was relieved to find the lack of apparent hostile presence, Corporal Winters and several of the other veteran troops were visibly jittery as they waited for the translator to finish questioning the headman. Noticing their agitation, Lieutenant Daniels took PFC Masters aside. "What's got you so jumpy, Corporal? Kit didn't find any evidence of enemy activity."

Tyler nodded, his fingers drumming a nervous tattoo on the grip and trigger guard of his ready-slung M60. "That's exactly what's got me on edge, Sir. If we had found booby traps, I'd say that either the VC weren't here, or else they were trying to keep the locals in line. With no traps, it either means that the locals have fallen in line and are working with the VC, or else that the VC are in the area and don't want/need booby traps to take care of us."

Lieutenant Daniels raised his eyebrows. "Take care of us? You mean they know where we are?"

Tyler nodded. "Lieutenant, they've probably had people watching us from he moment we stepped out the front gate of the airbase."

Lieutenant Daniels was about to comment on that, when the translator turned to him. "He says there were Cong in the area, but they are gone now; they have not been here for a few days."

Nodding, Lieutenant Daniels passed on his thanks to the headman, and began gathering his platoon back together preparatory to leaving. Pausing as they were about to head out, he conferred for a moment with Staff Sergeant Bellamy. "The headman says that the Cong were here, but that they are gone now, and have not been seen for several days."

Bellamy's face was grim. "Dat prob'ly mean de Cong be leavin' traps for us, and mebbe comin' back for us. I'll tell Kit, but you be keeping your eyes open for dem."

Swallowing his nervousness, Lieutenant Daniels nodded again, pulling his sidearm; a 1911 .45 caliber handgun; checking to make sure that the hammer was back with a round in the chamber and the safety was on. Satisfied that it was prepped correctly, he re-checked his M16, looking up to find Staff Sergeant Bellamy waiting for him. "De men be told, and dey be ready to move, Sir."

Nodding, Lieutenant Daniels holstered his 1911. "All right, let's go."

Turning to the platoon, Bellamy raised his voice. "Platoon, move out!"

Less than twenty minutes after they were clear of the

village, as they were moving along the edge of a rice paddy, Kit suddenly dropped to the ground. "Down, now!"

Bemused, Lieutenant Daniels nonetheless fell flat on his face as the rest of the platoon followed suit. A breathless heartbeat followed, with nothing happening, and he was about to ask what was going on when a cylinder of metal erupted from the earth where Kit had been standing, seeming to hover for an instant about a meter off the ground before exploding in a shower of shrapnel, sending metal rods flying in all directions. As the echoes of the explosion faded, Lieutenant Daniels raised his head. "What was that?"

Sergeant Powell took a cautious look around before rising to his feet. "Some kind of bouncing mine; probably a QZM-model from Russia."

Corporal Winters nodded, climbing back up onto the raised embankment. "Yeah. Fortunately it was on a standard pressure sensor, which can be felt if you're looking for it, or else we would all be dead."

As they got back into formation and began moving once again, there was a sudden burst of firing from the tree line on the opposite side of the paddy, and one of the men was hit by a burst of bullets in the chest and stomach, dropping to the ground in a heap. "Down, down, take cover!" shouted Lieutenant Daniels as he slid down the far side of the embankment. Taking a breath to calm himself, he poked his rifle up over the lip of the embankment and began firing his rifle at the invisible foe which now menaced them from across the waterlogged expanse of the rice paddy. Ceasing fire and rolling onto his back as his radio operator reached him, he grabbed the handset. "Steel Rain, Steel Rain, this is Dog One Six, do you read me, over?"

"Dog One Six, this is Steel Rain, go ahead."

"Steel Rain, I I am in heavy contact, request fire mission, Zulu Tango, Three-Six-Two, Three-Five-Zero,

Zero-Six-Two degrees, over."

Releasing the handset's 'talk' button, he waited, ducking as bullets zipped by overhead, and returning a hasty burst of shots. A brief moment passed, then the artillery Fire Direction Control Officer responded. "Roger that, Dog One Six. Shot, over; first one's smoke."

Lieutenant Daniels acknowledged the targeting shot with a terse, "Shot, out," and then waited. Thirty seconds later, the shell impacted a good one hundred yards 'under' the target, sending up a plume of smoke. Pressing the talk button again, Lieutenant Daniels spoke. "Up one hundred, fire for effect!"

"Up one hundred, roger."

A few more seconds followed, then almost a dozen shells came screaming in, plastering the area from whence the enemy fire had come with high explosive and shrapnel. A few moments passed, then Sergeant Powell stuck his head up for a second, bobbing it back down, then back up again. When nothing happened, he crawled up onto the embankment, and then waved an 'all-clear' to Lieutenant Daniels. Getting back on the radio, Daniels spoke. "Target destroyed, Steel Rain. Thanks."

"Roger, target destroyed. Steel Rain out."

Taking stock of the platoon, it was discovered that three men were dead, and another five wounded; though none critically. After another helicopter arrived to collect the dead, the platoon moved out, making their way to the suspected cache site, which turned up empty, and then heading back to base. Making it back without incident, they settled in to await the next round of replacements and the next mission. About two weeks after the patrol, Carl received yet another letter from Rhiannon; he had been receiving several of them at a time, but he could deduce from the postmarks that she was writing about one a week, as promised.

My Dear Carl,

I know you probably haven't had time to write back to me yet, but here's another letter. I had an interesting experience at the library the other day; a journalist came in looking for material on the abolitionists from the Civil War. I never thought about where journalists got their information and historical references from; I suppose I should have known they would come to a library for it, but I never gave it a second thought before now. Did you ever wonder where journalists got their historical information?

I don't really have much else to write about right now; things are fairly quiet here. Are things quiet over there?

Love,

Rhiann

Folding up the letter, Carl shook his head. It was most certainly not quiet; at least, while it had been relatively quiet for him and his platoon personally, the last two weeks had been spent conducting helicopter-borne 'search and destroy' missions similar to the foot patrol that his platoon had undertaken, but with helicopters ferrying the troops to known or suspected Viet Cong locations, and then encircling or pursuing the enemy they found in the area. Replacements were due in the next day or two, at which point Dog Company would be taking part in the missions again, deploying with a second platoon at minimum, and with the entirety of Dog Company if the mission warranted it; so far, no more than two platoons had been deployed at one time, but they were expecting an upswing in deployment strength as they began to find larger targets. If the past three deployments were any guide, they would be deploying in tandem with Third Platoon, as Second and Fourth had been the ones going out most recently.

The next day, they were brought back up to full strength by the arrival of fourteen replacements, and the day after that they were called into the briefing room with the rest of Dog Company. As the four platoons crowded in, Captain Morgan began the briefing. "All right, Intelligence has reported that approximately fifty or so Viet Cong are guarding a supply cache, here. We will be sending in Second and Third Platoon as a blocking force, deploying along the ridge line over here, and then landing elements of First Platoon along the other side of the position to overrun the Cong position and hopefully drive them into Second and Third Platoon's positions. You will be supported by UH-1 gunships, with an A-37 overhead on standby for Combat Air Support. Any questions?"

Lieutenant Kentworthy raised a hand. "How many transport Hueys are we using, Sir?"

Captain Morgan grimaced. "Unfortunately we only have twelve on station at the moment, so we can only transport two platoons at a time. We have two different Landing Zones, one on either side of the enemy cache site, and will be putting each platoon on the side nearest their engagement point to minimize travel time. The assault waves will be accompanied by two UH-1 gunships, which will then remain in the area. Transit time will be approximately fifteen minutes one way. Any other questions?"

No one answered, and he nodded. "All right then, grab your gear, and go with God. Second and Third Platoon, you're hitting the air in ten minutes."

Assembling in the staging area, Lieutenant Daniels and his platoon waited tensely as the men of Third and Fourth Platoon climbed aboard the helicopters, watching from behind their hands as the thrumming rotor blades kicked up a cloud of dust and debris, until they were over the horizon and the sound of the rotors had faded. The minutes passed in tense silence as they awaited the return of the choppers, wondering what fate had befallen their brother platoons in the jungles that had received them. Finally the sound of the returning helicopters reached their ears, and Lieutenant Daniels waved to his men. "All right, get ready to move!"

Making no move to obey the order, Corporal Winters shook his head. "Not so fast, Sir. They're going to have to refuel first, and that's going to take at least a few minutes; and during that time, I doubt the ground crews will want a bunch of infantry milling around, getting in the way and trying to get onto the choppers they're refueling. Better to wait until we get the go-ahead from the ground crew."

Sitting back down, Lieutenant Daniels nodded. "Got it. Thanks."

The minutes seemed to stretch forever, but finally, the

ground crew finished refueling, cleared the landing pad, and waved an 'all-clear' signal. Getting back on his feet, Lieutenant Daniels waved to his men again. "All right, let's go!"

Scrambling aboard the choppers, six men to a helicopter, they sat or crouched in the open bays, hanging onto anything that seemed stable or at least firmly attached as the helicopters rose into the air one after the other, pointing their noses in the direction of the enemy cache and speeding forward like giant insects, or birds of prey. The time seemed to both fly and crawl, the seconds oozing by like they were stuck in quicksand, but the minutes disappearing faster than the cinnamon rolls in the mess hall at breakfast time. All of a sudden, they were circling over the Landing Zone, and then they were on the deck. His boots thumping into the ground and sending a shock wave up his legs, Lieutenant Daniels dashed for the tree line, waving for his men to set up a perimeter as the helicopters began to lift off, having disgorged their deadly cargoes. Gathering into formation, the platoon began moving toward the cache location, about a kilometer from the Landing Zone. Stealth was less of a concern at this point; the enemy knew that they were there, and would be more than likely making ready to pull out and vanish into the jungle at this point; First Platoon's job was to catch them before that could happen, and that depended on moving faster than the Cong could. Their likely escape route had been screened by Second and Third, but if they engaged, it was First's job to move in behind them and catch them between two fires, as it were, as well as cutting off any retreat they might attempt once they figured out they were blocked. All but running through the jungle, they heard the sound of gunfire ripping through the trees ahead of them, interspersed with explosions, and the sudden buzzing thunder of a Mingun as the gunships engaged. Reaching the edge of the enemy encampment, one of the riflemen hit a Punji Deadfall; a framework of branches topped by heavy logs and layered along the bottom by deadly bamboo spikes; impaled and crushed, he was dead before his mortal remains finished hitting the ground. Slowing their pace as they began checking more carefully for traps and snares, the two platoons advanced through the encampment. Forty yards into the clearing, Lieutenant Daniels spotted a machine gun as the gunner scrambled to get his weapon trained on the raiders. "Down, get down!" he shouted, as he tackled the man to his right, landing the two of them behind a truck with a thud that knocked the wind out of him. A hail of bullets raked the air where he had been a second before, bullets reaching for the rest of First Platoon as they scrambled to find cover. Three men were hit, but not badly, and they quickly returned fire. Fighting for breath, Lieutenant Daniels coughed violently, finally sucking down a lungful of air after what seemed like a dozen lifetimes, pushing to his feet and firing over the hood of the truck. Fortunately, the gunner was distracted by his fire, and ducked, allowing one of the grenadiers to put a round on top of him. Settling the bipod of the M60 on a wall of sandbags the enemy had recently vacated, Lance Corporal Masters opened fire on a group of fleeing Viet Cong fighters, cutting them down in a spray of bullets. Lieutenant Daniels felt the old sensation of fear and adrenaline rising in his throat, but worked to clamp it down, focusing instead on where he would be moving; what was happening to his left and right with his men, and what the enemy was doing; trying to crowd out any thoughts of fear and panic by filling his mind with other thoughts. Slowly but steadily, they were advancing, pushing the enemy further north, into the trap set by Second and Third Platoons. So far, so good. Overhead, the UH-1C gunship tilted, hovering briefly as it launched a salvo of rockets into one of the buildings from which heavy enemy fire emanated. As the survivors of the blasts stumbled clear of the wreckage, the gunship mopped up with Minigun fire, mowing them down. Running forward to occupy the now-past-tense stronghold, the assault platoon opened fire on the few guerrillas who still stood and fought. As the firing slowed, then stopped from the enemy side, Lieutenant Daniels waved to his men. "Cease fire, cease fire!"

Passing on the order, Platoon Sergeant Bellamy waited, listening. Aside from a few scattered shots from Fourth Platoon's sector, and the thrum of rotor blades overhead, all was quiet. Turning to Bellamy, Lieutenant Daniels nodded. "Okay, Sergeant. Pop smoke; let 'em know it's safe."

Nodding acknowledgment, Platoon Sergeant Bellamy pulled a smoke grenade from his vest, tossing it away from the men and onto the rubble of what had been one of the main buildings. After a moment, red smoke began to billow upward, signaling that it was safe to bring in the two helicopters loaded with Combat Engineers to destroy the cache. Twenty minutes later, the Engineers were on the ground, laying charges to destroy the supplies found in the cache. Watching them assembling the equipment and setting plastic explosive around it, Lieutenant Daniels turned to Lance Corporal Masters. "Why are they destroying the rice? Wouldn't it make better sense to give it to the villagers?"

His expression sorrowful, Lance Corporal Masters shook his head. "As much as I'd like to say yes, in the long run, no. See, if we gave it to the villagers, the Cong would just come and get it back. This way, although the villagers don't get it, at least the Cong don't either."

Nodding comprehension, Lieutenant Daniels began walking back toward the helicopter, followed by the rest of his men. Miraculously, none had been injured, but the same could not be said of the other platoons. Third had three men killed and another eight wounded, and Second had six killed and four wounded. As the medevac choppers began landing, Lieutenant Daniels and his platoon moved into a defensive perimeter, eyes scanning the jungle for signs of threat as the wounded and dead were either loaded on stretchers or zipped into body bags and loaded onto the waiting helicopters. With that task accomplished, the battered company collapsed back to the transport choppers, loading up and heading for home. As they climbed off the helicopters, Lieutenant Kentworthy walked over. "So, that was your first airborne search and destroy mission. How do you feel?"

Wiping a hand across his face, which came away with a slick of sweat, smoke-grime, and dust, Lieutenant Daniels shook his head. "I don't exactly know."

He paused for a moment to collect his thoughts, then continued. "I guess...I guess I feel both good and bad. I mean, I feel good that we won, and we didn't have too many casualties, but I feel bad because it didn't seem like we did anything tangible. Sure, we destroyed a cache of supplies, and we racked up a seventy-five body count, but we aren't holding territory, we aren't capturing a specific objective, and we aren't involved in a full-scale invasion of North Vietnam."

He stopped, looking slightly embarrassed, but Lieutenant Kentworthy was nodding. "Yeah, I get it. A lot of the guys I talk to say the same thing; that we don't have a clear objective in this war, that this is turning into a war of attrition; and most if not all of the South Vietnamese people I've talked to or heard about agree with what you were saying; they want to invade North Vietnam, take Hanoi, and end this war in their favor."

Lieutenant Daniels looked incredulous. "So if that's what they want, then why aren't we doing just that? Why aren't we just launching a team north to take Hanoi and capture or kill Ho Chi Minh?"

Lieutenant Kentworthy looked grim. "I asked Captain Morgan about that one time. He told me that according to the politicians, launching an invasion of North Vietnam would draw Russia and China into the war, and alter this into a confrontation that could spark a thermonuclear war. I am inclined to doubt that, personally, but that's the word from Washington, so we try to rack the body count high enough that the North Vietnamese either run out of troops to fight us with, or else just cry Uncle."

Mulling over that concept, Lieutenant Daniels nodded. "Well, let's hope that they cry Uncle pretty soon."

Walking into the recreation hall, the two men spotted a fracas breaking out on the far side of the hall, and ran over to investigate, along with several other men already inside. Arriving at the scene, they found Sergeant First Class Lyman grappling with Captain Kemper; both mens' faces bright red; Captain Kemper from rage, and Sergeant First Class Lyman due to the fact that Captain Kemper's hands were locked around his throat and severely restricting his breathing. Without hesitation, Lieutenant Daniels jumped on Kemper's back, locking in a Full Nelson and rearing back to pull the enraged Captain's arms away from Lyman's throat. Straining to lift him and Sergeant First Class Lyman as Kemper refused to release his grip despite the pressure on his upper arms and shoulders, Daniels gasped at Lieutenant Kentworthy, "Get his hands off!"

Sliding in on his knees, Lieutenant Kentworthy grabbed Captain Kemper's thumbs, one in each hand, and began levering them away from Lyman's trachea as he half-turned to the few men standing uncertainly by the door. "Get Lieutenant Colonel Schumacher, you dolts! MOVE!"

As they scrambled for the door, Lieutenant Kentworthy managed to get one of Captain Kemper's hands clear of SFC Lyman's throat, almost dislocating the thumb in the process. Both hands latching onto Captain Kemper's wrist, Sergeant First Class Lyman began pulling the other hand away. Without SFC Lyman's weight holding him down, Lieutenant Daniels was able to lift the raging officer clear of his opponent, receiving a kick in the shins for his troubles. As he was kicked again, he shifted his hold, wrapping his arms around Captain Kemper's shoulders and spinning him around. As Captain Kemper tried to punch him, he slipped the blow, one arm threading under Kemper's shoulder as the other shot over his other shoulder. Grabbing Kemper's upper arm with the hand over the shoulder, Lieutenant Daniels stepped in and to one side, pulling with his hand as his other arm pushed upward hard against Kemper's shoulder, and simultaneously dropped to the ground, rolling backwards and throwing Kemper across his body, landing on top. As Captain Kemper wheezed for breath, the wind knocked out of him by the throw, Lieutenant Colonel Schumacher appeared in the doorway, flanked by the two men who had gone to get him. "What's going on here?"

Looking up guiltily, Lieutenant Daniels scrambled to his feet as Lieutenant Kentworthy helped Sergeant First Class Lyman to his feet. He was about to explain when Lieutenant Kentworthy spoke up, his voice crisp and official. "Lieutenant Daniels and I walked in on an altercation between Captain Kentworthy and Sergeant First Class Lyman; the reason for the altercation remains to be explained. It was immediately obvious to both of us that Sergeant First Class Lyman's life was in peril, and therefore we intervened, and sent men to go get you as quickly as possible."

He paused for the briefest of instants to look over at Carl, surprised respect in his eyes, before continuing. "Lieutenant Daniels was able to subdue Captain Kemper just as you arrived."

Nodding, Lieutenant Colonel Schumacher looked from one face to the next in silence for a long moment, stopping on Sergeant First Class Lyman's face, which bore several bruises and a wide abrasion on the jawline. "Do you concur with Lieutenant Kentworthy's statement, Sergeant?"

Nodding painfully, Jimmy spoke, his voice a hoarse

rasp. "Yes, Sir. I do."

Turning to Captain Kemper, who was beginning to breathe normally again, Lieutenant Colonel Schumacher continued. "Captain? What was the nature of the disagreement that you and Sergeant First Class Lyman, and who started the fighting?"

Trying to sit up, Captain Kemper grabbed onto a nearby table for support. "We were playing poker, Sir, with a couple of the other guys, and Lyman here cheated. I called him on it, but nobody else would believe me. So, after trying to prove it verbally, I decided to prove it by finding the cards he was hiding. He didn't like that idea, so he tried to stop me. Things got physical at that point; I don't remember who actually started fighting."

Private Korman, one of the men who had been sent for Schumacher, spoke up, his voice hesitant. "It was kind of a mutual thing, Sir. When Captain Kemper went after Lyman and started trying to find cards in his sleeves, Sergeant Lyman pushed his hand away, and then they both kind of started wrestling and punching each other. Then the Captain started choking Sergeant Lyman, yelling about how he was gonna teach him to cheat at poker, and then Lieutenant Daniels and Lieutenant Kentworthy showed up."

He stopped, and Lieutenant Colonel Schumacher turned to face him. "Go on, Private."

Private Korman cleared his throat nervously and then continued. "Well, Sir, Lieutenant Kentworthy started trying to get the Captain's hands off of Sergeant Lyman's neck, and Lieutenant Daniels started wrestling with the Captain, trying to pull him away. Then Lieutenant Kentworthy yelled for us to go get you, and we…did, Sir."

Nodding, Lieutenant Colonel Schumacher turned to Captain Kemper. "Captain, I'll speak with you in my office. The rest of you, dismissed."

As Private Korman turned to go, he spoke. "Not you, Private. Wait a minute."

Swallowing hard, Private Korman waited while the rest of the men left, and Lieutenant Colonel Schumacher shut the door. "All right, Private, I want the truth. Was Sergeant First Class Lyman actually cheating at the poker table?"

Private Korman shook his head vigorously. "No, Sir! He didn't have any cards up his sleeve, and I was watching him every time he dealt. He, well, no offense to the Sergeant, Sir, but he's just not fast enough in the hands to do a dirty deal. He may be a chess whiz, but he's just not very good at that side of cards."

Lieutenant Colonel Schumacher pursed his lips thoughtfully for a moment, then nodded. "All right, Private, thank you. Dismissed."

Over in Schumacher's office, Captain Kemper stood at Parade Rest as Lieutenant Colonel Schumacher walked in, pacing thoughtfully as he rolled a fat Cuban cigar through the flame of his lighter. "Captain, this is not the first time you've been in a situation warranting disciplinary action for reckless and uncontrolled behavior; be it fighting with both officers and enlisted men, taking action without following proper protocol, or administering unwarranted disciplinary action. Did any of the other poker players see or suspect that Sergeant Lyman was cheating?"

His face sullen, Captain Kemper shook his head. "No, Sir. But I knew he was, even if no one else would believe me. I just knew he was."

Lieutenant Colonel Schumacher took a thoughtful drag on his cigar, talking with the smoke. "I see. You just knew, and so you just let go and pitched into him, determined that you were right; so determined, in fact, that you couldn't even keep good enough control of yourself to take it to proper channels."

He paused to take another drag, then looked directly at

Captain Kemper for the first time since entering his office. "You know what I know, Bill? You're a fool. You just don't have any control over yourself, and that lack of control is going to get good men under your command killed. I'm not going to let that happen, Bill; I simply can't. Now, if this were the first time this sort of thing had happened, or if you weren't of the personality you are and were trying to change your approach to dealing with conflict, I could be tempted to let it slide, and just try to smooth things over, but this is the sixth time this has happened, and you aren't showing any sign of even wanting to change how you deal with problems. Therefore, I am going to have to submit you for court-martial."

***

Handing Sergeant First Class Lyman another hot compress, Lieutenant Kentworthy gave a small grin. "Feeling any better, Jimmy?"

Swallowing with difficulty, Sergeant First Class set the mug of tea down and pressed the hot compress gently against his aching throat. "Sure, sure. Now, instead of feeling like I'm being choked to death, I feel like I was just choked to death. I'd say that's an improvement, Sir."

Waving him to silence, Lieutenant Daniels rose to grab the tea mug, heading for the kitchen to top it off. "Don't try to talk; just rest your throat and keep drinking the tea; it'll help your throat heal."

As he returned with the freshened mug, Lieutenant Kentworthy gave him a sidelong glance. "That was some interesting moves you put on the Captain back there. What was that, anyway?"

Lieutenant Daniels shrugged. "I was on the high school wrestling team; not to brag, but I helped lead our team to victory at the State Championships three years running. My coach said that we could have had a shot at nationals my senior year, and that with some more training, I could have gone professional."

Lieutenant Kentworthy was silent for a moment, and then asked, "So why didn't you? Why did you join the Army instead?"

Carl shrugged. "I figured that I should do something for my country after all it had done for me, and this seemed to be the best way to do that. Plus, I ran into an Army Recruiter who told me all about the Airborne, and what a proud history it had, and how amazing it would be to join the Airborne, and all the benefits of it, and he made it sound so cool, I just figured, why not? Of course, that was before I met Rhiannon, but I'm still glad that I joined."

Pulling out the picture of Rhiannon, he cradled it in his palm. Clearing his throat, Sergeant First Class Lyman spoke. "Well, Sir, I'm really glad you joined the Army."

Pitching his voice into a cracked falsetto, he continued. "Oh, yes, darling, I'm sooo glad you were able to combine your career choices out there in Vietnam. Just think, you can be in the Army and be a professional wrestler; it's the best of both worlds!"

Brow furrowing in confusion as Lieutenant Kentworthy burst out laughing, Carl finally caught on to the fact that Jimmy was talking as though he was Rhiannon, and cracked a grin. "Cute, Sarge. Real cute. Now seriously, rest your voice, man."

The rest of the week, and the one following, was spent quietly, mostly trying to avoid talking about the incident at the recreation hall and ensuing court-martial that had followed, leading to Captain Kemper being demoted to Lieutenant and rotated out of combat service. However, by the third week, Dog Company was heading back out again with Charlie Company on a search-and-destroy mission, this time aiming to screen a province that had been reporting an uptick in VC presence. The mission briefing was simple. "Dog Company will be airlifted in and form a screening force that will advance through the province in order to discover and destroy any Viet Cong presence in the area. Charlie will likewise be airlifted in, but they will form a blocking force on the far side to cut off any Viet Cong retreat towards the border. Good luck gentlemen."

As they began packing their gear, Lieutenant Daniels drew Lieutenant Kentworthy aside. "Mark, I've got a question. How come when it was just me and First Platoon going out on a search and destroy mission, I got a nuts-and-bolts briefing from Captain Morgan that I then had to flesh out for my men, but now that everyone's coming along, we get our briefings directly from either Captain Morgan or Lieutenant Colonel Schumacher? And here's another one: Why was my first mission a one-platoon march through the jungle with orders to chase any opposition I came up against to ground, but now we're going out with two or three platoons minimum, and having a blocking force on one side with the other half of the team pushing the Cong into the blocking force?"

Lieutenant Kentworthy shrugged. "Ask the Cong. They've started showing themselves in greater numbers in our area, so we need larger forces to take 'em on. As to the tactics, Captain Morgan didn't know exactly how many or where they were when you went out, so he just sent you to check on the villages and collect intelligence on the enemy's whereabouts."

Lieutenant Daniels looked confused. "But most of the villages didn't know where the Cong were. At the one village, they didn't give us a chance to ask, and at the other one, they said they weren't there now but that they had been there a few days ago; and it turned out that they had come back to get us."

Lieutenant Kentworthy nodded. "True, but at the other villages that told us where the Cong weren't. Have you noticed that the two missions we've been on or are prepped for since your patrol have been in the same general area of the village that your report said the Cong were still present?"

Lieutenant Daniels considered that for a moment, then frowned. "Okay, but here's another question. Why is Dog Company always the one playing 'hammer' in this scenario? Why don't they put us in the blocking force position once in a while?"

Lieutenant Kentworthy smirked. "Well, that's a bit of a generalization, considering that this is the second mission we've been on that we've been placed as a blocking force since you got here, but the answer may be that they think we're good enough at that job to keep us there. Take it as a possible compliment to your jungle-fighting skills, as well as those of the rest of the company."

Further conversation was cut off by the Platoon Sergeant of Kentworthy's platoon, a leather-faced veteran with a close-cropped shock of graying hair and hard blue eyes, named Ed Piper. Teeth clenched around his perpetual cigar, Platoon Sergeant Piper strode up to the two men, looking from one to the other as salutes were exchanged. "Lieutenant, the platoon is ready to move. Lieutenant Daniels, Sergeant Bellamy asked me to notify you that First Platoon is preparing to board the helicopters."

Returning the salute, Lieutenant Kentworthy extended his hand to Lieutenant Daniels. "Thank you, Sergeant, I'm right behind you. Good luck, Carl. See you on the ground."

Climbing aboard the helicopter, Lieutenant Daniels tried not to fidget as he watched the air base grow smaller and then disappear from his field of vision. Staring down at the jungle below, he was jolted from his reverie by a poke in the shoulder. Turning, he saw one of the new replacements, a tanned, muscled young man nicknamed 'Surfer', proffering a pack of gum. "Gum, Sir? Always helps me when I'm nervous."

Nodding his thanks, Lieutenant Daniels accepted a stick, popping it in his mouth and chewing rapidly. The Landing Zone swooped into view; a wide, flat clearing with long grass dominating the open space. Turning in his seat, the co-pilot raised his voice to compete with the thrumming of the rotors and the thunder of the M60 machine guns hosing the tree line. "Be advised, ladies, this is gonna be a hot landing zone, so keep your heads down once you get out there!"

Raising a hand to acknowledge, Lieutenant Daniels gripped his M16 and gave Platoon Sergeant Bellamy and his radioman a thumbs-up, which they returned; Sergeant Bellamy with a reassuring grin, the young radio operator giving a shaky grimace as he attempted to return the grin. Jumping out as the Huey 'bounced', pulling up into a hover a few feet off the ground, the men began running for the tree line, making it almost halfway there before the first enemy fire began to chatter and crack from the undergrowth. Five men went down in the first few seconds, and the survivors hit the deck to return fire. Grabbing the radio, Captain Morgan began calling in an artillery strike. "Steel Rain, Steel Rain, this is Dog Six. Fire Mission, Papa November, Zero-Eight-Four, Zero-Five-Three, Zero-Six-Two degrees; gooks in the tree line."

Firing his M16 at the muzzle flashes he could see, Lieutenant Daniels heard the 'bloop' of the M79 firing to his left, followed a few seconds later by the explosion in the tree line. Noticing several of his men starting to get up, he yelled, "Negative, get your heads down! Let the arty deal with it; don't get yourselves killed for nothing!"

Most of them heard him, dropping back down or tackling the two who didn't to the ground, barely avoiding a vicious burst of machine gun fire that tracked the spot they had been. As Captain Morgan walked the artillery onto the targets, the enemy firing abruptly ceased, the explosions of the artillery rounds fading into an eerie silence as the company held its fire to check effect. After a moment, Captain Morgan stood, waving the company forward, advancing at a cautious walk. Reaching the blasted and smoking trees, they began probing for signs of the enemy, finding none until almost a kilometer and a half into the jungle, when they discovered a hastily laid mine along the trail; the dirt still moist when Kit probed the area. Planting a warning signal alongside it, they moved forward, more cautiously than their original advance had been. Suddenly Kit raised a fist, dropping to one knee beside the trail where he had been ranging ahead of the platoon. Moving forward, Sergeant Bellamy knelt beside him. "What is it, Corporal?"

Pointing forward and to the left, Kit indicated a group of Viet Cong about three hundred yards away, moving toward them at a rapid but cautious pace. "They must have spotted the blocking force and scooted for here, but they didn't know we were coming; or else they didn't care, and just decided to try to ambush us."

Sergeant Bellamy snorted. "Den dey be in for a surprise."

Rising to his feet, he walked back over to where Lieutenant Daniels was waiting, the rest of the platoon kneeling nearby. "What is it, Sergeant?"

"Well, Sir, de Cong are comin' dis way; Kit is no sure if dey are trying to ambush us, or if dey just runnin' from de other group."

Nodding, Lieutenant Daniels motioned to Lieutenant Kentworthy, who was standing a few yards away. "Mark, get over here!"

Quickly passing on the information, he pointed in the direction Sergeant Bellamy had indicated. "Should we let Captain Morgan know, or just ambush them ourselves?"

Lieutenant Kentworthy nodded. "Both. Start moving your platoon over to block where they're coming through, and I'll notify Captain Morgan and then move my platoon to reinforce you."

Lieutenant Daniels jogged back to his platoon, informing them of the plan. Waving an arm at the men, Sergeant Bellamy began following Lieutenant Daniels through the undergrowth. "Allons!"

Most of the men got to their feet and began tramping after Lieutenant Daniels and Sergeant Bellamy, but one of the new recruits stayed put, staring after Bellamy in confusion. "What did he say?"

With an impatient sigh, Private Turner grabbed the newcomer by his backpack and hustled him along. "He said 'go', but he sometimes says things in Cajun. You gotta learn some of the words he uses; or else just do what the rest of the platoon is doing, okay?"

Stealthily deploying along a line ahead of where the Viet Cong were coming, the platoon set up a hasty ambush: Masters and the M60 on one flank with a handful of the riflemen, Holland and the M79 on the other flank with three or four riflemen as security, and the rest of the men deployed to screen the mortar. As they waited tensely for the enemy to enter the killing zone, Lieutenant Kentworthy sprinted over to where Captain Morgan was conferring with Lieutenant Seybold, the commander of Second Platoon, about the advance to the right flank. "Captain Morgan, Sir! First Platoon has discovered a hostile element, and is moving to ambush them now. I have promised reinforcement from Third Platoon as soon as I inform you of what is happening!"

Mind racing, Captain Morgan turned to Lieutenant Seybold. "Belay that idea, Seybold; tell Lieutenant Newark to move only far enough to secure the position until we get a report from First and Third; then we'll move to continue the advance along the line at the flank."

Turning back to Lieutenant Kentworthy, he continued. "As soon as you've terminated the enemy force, notify me, understood?"

Nodding, Lieutenant Kentworthy saluted, and then dashed back to his platoon. "Move out! As soon as First engages, take the Cong in the flank and move to encircle them!"

As the Viet Cong moved forward, Lieutenant Daniels wiped his sweating palms on his pant legs, one eye on the advancing foe, the other on Corporal Winters, who would be signaling the start of the ambush. Closer, and closer still the enemy came, and still no signal. Then, just as Lieutenant Daniels was about to go ahead and open fire, thinking that Corporal Winters had been taken out, a grenade burst in the midst of the enemy, taking out three of them in a blast of fury; the signal for the ambush to begin. Ducking briefly at the blast, Lieutenant Daniels began firing into the mass of enemy, more explosions shaking the ground as the M79 and mortar added their voices to the raging firefight. As the enemy began to return fire, the ones on the flank and rear began to drop as automatic fire crackled out of the jungle. "Cease fire, cease fire!" shouted Lieutenant Daniels as the last of the enemy dropped to the ground; a few more shots rang out from the other side of the ambush, finishing off the wounded or faking, and then silence reigned again in the immediate vicinity; broken by a brief spate of small-arms fire in the distance as the blocking force was engaged by another group of Viet Cong. Moving out of cover, Lieutenant Kentworthy motioned to one of his men. "Notify Captain Morgan that the enemy force has been terminated with extreme prejudice."

As the Private saluted and scampered off through the brush, Lieutenant Kentworthy surveyed the positioning of the ambush force. "Well done, Carl. You're learning fast."

Nodding his thanks, Lieutenant Daniels swapped his empty magazine for a full one, tapping the forward assist. "Thanks. You didn't do so bad yourself."

Checking on the status of the platoon, it was discovered that they had suffered two bullet grazes, but no further injuries. Re-forming the skirmish line, they continued their advance, turning up further evidence of enemy presence: booby traps, dead campfires, and lesser caches of supplies, but no further enemy soldiers. Finally, they came into contact with the men of Charlie Company; concluding the search and destroy mission with a body count of almost two hundred and eighty, and six hundred pounds of supplies captured and destroyed.

With the highest body count of the month, both Dog and Charlie Company were permitted a weekend pass in Saigon for R&R. Many of the men were ecstatic, making plans for bar-hopping and a stay in a hotel with real beds and room service, but Lieutenant Daniels, while glad to get out of the airbase and enjoy some civilized accommodations for a change, was not looking forward to being in Saigon. For one thing, alcohol held no draw for him; he had gotten drunk one time in high school when his friends had swiped some beer and he had joined in the 'fun', and it was not an experience he wished to repeat; and for another, being away from the danger and tension of combat made him think about Rhiannon, which depressed him. Nonetheless, he agreed to come, if only to keep an eye on his friends and make sure that they minimized their stupidity. Walking down the main avenue of Saigon's downtown section, he shook his head as the little group consisting of Lieutenant Kentworthy, Corporal Winters, Sergeant Bellamy, Private First Class Masters, and Sergeant First Class Lyman turned toward yet another club. Following them in, he paused for a moment to transfer a twenty-dollar bill to his shirt pocket and let his eyes adjust; he was sending most of his pay home to Rhiannon, but he kept some back for an occasion like this, and it was better to pay from the stash he had allocated for this club than to haul out his wallet and find himself broke by the morning. By the time he had caught up to the group, they had already hit the bar; Mark, Tyler, and Jimmy already had cocktails in front of them, Roland was pouring a beer into a glass, and Kit had wandered off toward one of the side rooms where they were holding a Savate match; his interests lay in betting on the various, more violent sports hosted on the down-low by the clubs they were visiting, and he had suggested this one because it hosted Savate matches with a group of fighters who had stayed behind after the French pullout. Sidestepping a waitress, he joined the rest of the group at the bar, raising his voice to be heard over the music thumping from the dance floor. "Virgin Pina Colada."

Tyler, who had overheard what he said, looked at him in surprise. "How long have you been ordering non-alcoholic drinks?"

Letting his eyes bounce quickly over the group as he shifted sideways on the stool, Carl shrugged. "All night; why?"

Taking another sip from his own glass; whiskey on the rocks from the look of it; Tyler gave a shrug of his own. "I dunno. I just didn't notice; that's all."

Accepting the glass from the bartender with a nod of thanks, Carl took an appreciative sip, letting his gaze move from the dance floor, where Mark had summoned sufficient courage of the Dutch variety to venture out onto the floor with a young lady he had met from across the room; to the men at the bar, who were currently in the process of striking up a spirited conversation with a pair of Marines and a familiar-looking infantryman who had just walked in, to the door to the Savate match where Kit had vanished off to. Sliding his drink off of the bar, he carried it over to where the men were talking. As he approached, the familiar looking infantryman turned, and Carl recognized Private Aaron Turner, one of the men in his platoon. Recognizing him, Private Turner, who was clearly very drunk, drew himself up and gave Carl an exaggerated salute, his voice badly slurred, despite his attempts at deliberate pronunciation. "Good evening, Sir. Having a g-good time, at this, fine establishment?"

Returning the salute, Carl nodded. "At ease, Private. Yes, I am, thank you. Who are your jarhead friends?"

With a lopsided grin, Aaron clapped a friendly, if quite uncoordinated, arm around each of the men, one of whom was even drunker than Turner, the other obviously on his way and getting there with great gusto. "These are my good brothers-in-arms, Sir; my fellow killers."

Brow furrowing, Carl looked sharply at him. "Excuse me, Private?"

His cheerful demeanor slipping away, replaced by a mournful expression, Private Turner nodded. "Yes, Sir, we are killers. What we do out there, is no more than murder."

Suddenly his face crumpled, and he began sobbing. "Oh, Father in Heaven have mercy, what have I done? What have I done? All those men and women, murdered! How can I face my Maker with this on my soul?"

Staring helplessly from face to face, Carl spread his hands in confusion. "What on Earth is he talking about?"

Looking up from his highball, a Coke and Rum, Mark shook his head sadly. "He's talking about the fighting on the search and destroy patrols. He's fighting because he has orders to do so, but he's convinced that it's murder, and that he's going to Hell because of what he's done."

Grabbing Aaron by the shoulder, Carl pulled him around to look him in the eye. "Private, listen to me! What you've done out there in the jungle; the people you've killed, that's not murder!"

Confusion seeping through the guilt and grief on his face, Private Turner swiped at his eyes and tilted his head questioningly. "What do you mean, Sir? I-I, murdered them."

Shaking his head, Carl continued. "No, you didn't.

You see, what you're doing out there is killing as part of a war. If you were here in Saigon, or back home just walking around killing people who weren't trying to hurt you, just whacking them because you felt like it, that's murder; whereas when you kill in the jungle, they would kill you if you didn't kill them; that's not against the law in the Bible. Think, Private. Did God punish the people of Israel for killing in the wars that they were in? No. I'm not saying this is holy war, but it is war. You got nothing to feel guilty about, Private."

Turning to the bartender, he raised a finger. As the bartender hurried over, he cast a quick glance over at the less drunk Marine. "What have you guys been drinking?"

Puzzled, the Marine replied, "Um, I've been having, um, Scotch and Soda, he's been having Rusty Nails, and I've been having beer. Why?"

Ignoring the question, Carl addressed the waiter. "One Scotch and Soda, a beer, and can you make a Rusty Nail?"

Nodding, the bartender, a short, bony man of obvious French descent, moved away to prepare the drinks. Turning back to Aaron, he spoke. "Okay, you and your friends have a drink, and then head back to your hotel, okay?"

Nodding, Private Turner and the two Marines threw a trio of wobbling salutes, which Carl returned, and then turned their attention to the forthcoming drinks as Carl moved to sit next to Roland, who was in the process of pouring a second beer into his glass, watching intently as the foam rose, then receded. As he took a long swallow, Carl spoke. "Um, the guys are getting kind of smashed; don't you think we should call it a night pretty soon?"

Shaking his head, Roland grinned. "Non, my friend. Laissez les bon temps roulez."

Looking bemused, Carl glanced briefly at the grinning bartender before asking, "Sorry, what?"

With an apologetic smile, Roland took another swallow

of beer. "Means 'let de good times roll.' Comprendre?"

Carl blinked, taking a sip of his own drink. "Um, yes, and no. I mean, I'm pretty sure that what you just said is something about understanding, so; I guess I understand."

As Roland laughed, Carl continued, his voice startled. "I just realized, I never got the names of Aaron's buddies. Did you happen to catch them?"

His expression pensive, Roland thought about it for a moment, then nodded. "Well, I got de one's name, but the other one, he didn't talk too clear. He walk in, and he say something to me, and I thought he was a bit pa tous la, but den I learned he been to de bar before he get here, and I think, 'Nah, he just cassed.' But I didn't get his name."

Carl looked blank. "Okay, what did you just say? 'pah too la? Casceyed?"

Roland looked disgusted. "Non, et non, et non! I say pa tous la; 'not all there; a little crazy mebbe. Den, he cassed; he have too much to drink; he, ah, 'smashed'. Comprendre?"

Carl hesitated, then nodded. "Sure, yeah; I got it. I think."

Taking another sip of his drink, he grinned as he watched Mark dancing; the Dutch courage might have gotten him out on the dance floor, but he had had several drinks at the club they had visited earlier in the evening, and it was affecting his balance, with the result that he kept almost falling over, and frequently breaking his fall either on his partner or other dancers; but so far no one seemed to mind. "I wonder if he ever learned to dance before now, or if he's just making stuff up as he goes? Personally, my money's on the latter."

Grinning, Roland signaled for another beer. "Talk about."

Carl nodded. Roland had already used that one on him; explaining that it was a Cajun colloquialism of assent or agreement, not meaning that anyone was actually talking about anything. After getting another virgin Pina Colada, he decided to go check on Kit. Turning to the rest of the group, he tapped Tyler on the shoulder. "I'll be right back; don't leave just yet, okay?"

As Tyler nodded, he skirted the dance floor and pushed through the door leading to the fight area. As he closed the door behind him, the crowd roared with mixed approval and disappointment as one of the fighters landed a kick that knocked his opponent to the ground with a bleeding gash in his cheek. Snaking through the jostling, sweating crowd, he spotted Kit standing next to the bookie, his eyes fixed on the fighters. In the two days they had been in Saigon, he had only gone to clubs that had some kind of fight club, whether legal or off-the-books; usually only getting a single glass of arak, he would join the throng in the fight club area, betting heavily on the matches. Usually he was quite successful, but there had been three occasions on the previous evening where he had lost almost a thousand dollars. Carl had never asked him what the particular draw to the matches was, but he could see that Kit took pleasure both in the betting, and in watching the fights, whether or not he won. From the look on his face, he was both ahead, and backing the winning fighter, so Carl waited until the bout was over, and Kit was collecting his winnings before walking over. As he approached, Kit shuffled quickly through the bills he was given, frowned, and grabbed the bookie by the shoulder, evidently disputing the amount he had been given. Pushing aside a fat man in a business suit, Carl stepped into the conversation. "Is there a problem here?"

Turning, Kit relaxed marginally as he recognized Carl. "Yes, Sir. This guy is trying to cheat me. I should have gotten six hundred dollars, but I only got three hundred."

Waving his hands, the bookie shook his head. "No, no!

You only pay one hundred; odds three to one! Go away!"

Laying a hand on Kit's shoulder, Carl pulled gently. "Kit, he probably just doesn't remember; come on, we've got to be back at base tomorrow."

Shaking his head, Kit stood his ground. "No, Sir; I'm not leaving until I get my three hundred dollars. He has it; he's just trying to chisel me."

Face reddening, the bookie continued his arm-waving. "No, I am honest man; you have your money!"

Carl kept pulling Kit's shoulder. "Corporal, it's just money; it's not worth getting into a fight over. Come on."

As they turned to leave, the bookie kept yelling. "Go, go home thief!"

Kit almost turned to punch him, but Carl spotted him beginning to move in that direction and preempted the move by planting his palm on Kit's shoulder blade and preventing him from turning as he pushed him towards the exit. "Nope, only a fool answers the taunt of another fool. Come on, let's grab the guys and get out of here."

Pushing a simmering Kit ahead of him, Carl tapped Mark on the shoulder. "Lieutenant, I hate to be a buzz-kill, but we've got to be back at base in the morning; we'd best get moving."

Nodding, Mark turned to his dance partner, doffing an exaggerated and slightly unsteady bow. "A pleasure dancing with you, my dear; I hope, should I return to Saigon, that I shall have the pleasure again."

Jimmy was almost completely under the table, and Kit ended up hoisting him into a fireman's carry and carrying him out as Carl assisted Tyler out to the waiting cab. The buses to transport them back to the base were waiting at 0700 the next morning, and while most of the men were complaining about splitting headaches, they managed to make it in one piece back to the airbase. Sipping a cup of coffee, Mark shook his head, then winced at the brief motion. "How you can be so cheerful after all the drinking you did is beyond me, buddy."

Grinning, Carl stirred sugar into his own coffee. "Well, I didn't drink alcohol. I had non-alcoholic versions of the ones I was drinking."

Mark carefully raised one eyebrow. "Oh? Why is that?"

Carl shrugged, taking a tentative taste of his coffee. Deciding that it needed more sugar, he grimaced and reached for another sugar packet. "Well, for one thing, I didn't want a hangover; for another, I figured that at least one of us should have a clear head while out on the town; just in case something happened."

Mark gave a slight nod. "Okay; well, I guess, thanks?"

Carl waved a hand. "Don't mention it."

Things were fairly quiet for the next few weeks, with one or two patrols yielding a modest body count, but more often than not turning up mostly empty; however, rumblings of a bigger operation were traversing the grapevine of the camp. By the first week of November, the entire 173rd Airborne Brigade was called up to reinforce the Task Force operating in the Tay Ninh Province as part of Operation Attleboro. The nuts and bolts of the operation for the men of Dog Company were fairly similar to the missions they had been running up until that point, with helicopter-borne sweeps attempting to surprise the enemy positions, and as often as not hitting a hastily-abandoned camp or supply dump. By the time that they were committed, the operation was almost over, and in two weeks, they were back at Bien Hoa airbase, waiting for the next big operation as they sent out patrols in the area surrounding the base. As Christmas approached, Carl received a large box in the mail from Rhiannon. Carrying it back to the base, he set it on his bunk and opened the letter on top marked READ THIS FIRST!

Folding the letter back up, Carl slid it into the envelope, placing it into an empty ammunition crate he had requisitioned for the purpose of keeping Rhiannon's correspondence safe and sound, and then turned his attention to the box. On top was a pair of smaller boxes, each containing a large plum pudding, and a tin covered in brown paper; on closer inspection, the true label revealed that it was brandy sauce for the pudding. The next item out of the box was another tin, this one containing frosted Christmas cookies. As he lifted a bag marked To

My Dear Carl,

While I am very sad that we can't spend our first Christmas as a married couple together, I am proud of what you are doing over there. That said, I don't think that you should have to spend Christmas without a few comforts of home, so I put together some stuff that I hope will help you feel more Christmas-y over there. Also, from your letters, I feel I know the likes and dislikes of some of your friends over there to put in some things for them as well.

Merry Christmas, my darling, and a Happy New Year.

All my love,
Rhiannon

Mr. Bellamy; Merry Christmas! he frowned thoughtfully, then checked the back of the letter, finding a list of names. With a smile, Carl went to the door of the barracks. "Hey, Bellamy, grab Lieutenant Kentworthy, Corporal Winters, Sergeant Lyman, and Lance Corporal Masters and meet me in the barracks!"

His bewildered expression lost on Carl's back as he pivoted and headed back to his bunk, Sergeant Bellamy shrugged and went to go find the men requested. Diving back into the box, Carl found the packages addressed to the men he had summoned, and laid them on their bunks before turning as the door to the barracks opened to reveal the gaggle of befuddled men he had sent for. "You wanted to see us, Sir?"

Nodding, Carl repressed a grin. "Yes, Corporal. Each of you go stand by your beds and tell me what you find there."

Exchanging glances that said without words that they all clearly thought the commander of First Platoon had lost his mind, the men obeyed, skepticism giving way to wondering confusion as they picked up the packages he had laid out. Turning to face him, Sergeant Lyman held up the square package he had found. "Sir, what is this?"

Carl smiled. "Well, I mentioned each of you in my letters to my wife, and she decided to send each of you a Christmas present. I know Christmas isn't until tomorrow, but I figured, why not? Go ahead, open 'em up."

As the wrapping paper fell away, Sergeant Bellamy held up a bag of authentic Cajun seasoning; Sergeant Lyman cradled a folding travel chess set, Corporal Winters gazed admiringly at a miniature statue representing the Maltese Falcon; one of his favorite movies as well as his favorite book series, Lance Corporal Masters held an autographed baseball from the New York Yankees; his preferred team, and Lieutenant Kentworthy ran a hand across the cover of a copy of Songbirds of America; an avid birdwatcher, he had often spoken of his love of the pastime to Carl. "Carl, I...I don't know what to say. I mean..."

Carl grinned crookedly. "How about, 'Merry Christmas' to start with?"

As the men offered their thanks, he waved a hand. "Don't mention it, guys. I'll tell Rhiannon you appreciated it. Merry Christmas."

After they had left, he returned to the box, reaching down to the bottom, where two more packages addressed to him were nestled. Opening them, he found a locket with a picture of Rhiannon and a lock of her hair inside, and a bone-handled knife engraved with both of their initials inside a heart on one side, and the words Psalms 18:34 on the other side. Pulling out his correspondence box, he began writing, munching on one of the cookies.

My Dear Rhiannon,

Merry Christmas, darling. I got your letter, and you box this afternoon; I share your grief and disappointment at being apart for our first Christmas together, but I thank you for your support. I was going to wait until tomorrow to give the boys your presents, but then I thought, 'Nah, just do it today.' They loved them, and send their wholehearted thanks and appreciation. I cannot fully express on paper how deeply I appreciated the gifts you sent me, but I'll do my best. The locket now stays next to my heart, and every time I feel it, I think of you, and feel almost as if you are here with me; if only in spirit, and it reminds me of why I am fighting. I still miss you deeply, but your gift makes the distance just a tiny little bit more bearable, and the time go a little bit faster. By the way, the cookies are amazing; as is the plum pudding.

I have to go, the evening service will be starting in a few minutes. When I attend the service, I will say a prayer for you, and imagine you are sitting next to me.

All my love,
Carl.

After the service, he called Mark and the men of First Platoon back to the barracks, sharing out the plum pudding and cookies in a private little party with the men who had become his brothers over the past few months. The next day, the base held a Christmas Party, with military-issue plum pudding, turkey, and an exchange of simple gifts among the men, but that little gathering in the barracks, savoring the taste of homemade cooking by candlelight, held a special place in the hearts and memories of the men of First Platoon. The next couple of days were quiet, with no patrols, and Carl expressed his surprise over that fact to Tyler. "Why aren't we out there patrolling? Is something going on?"

Nodding, Tyler began shuffling the deck of cards he was practicing with; everyone knew he could trick-deal as well as any Vegas dealer; after the war, he was planning to go to Vegas to work at one of the casinos; so nobody played for money, but some of the men enjoyed trying to catch how he did it, as well as learning a few simple card tricks from him. "Yeah, the Tet Truce. It's a thing we do with the North Vietnamese every year at the Vietnamese new year; Tet. We don't fight them during the celebrations around this time, and they don't bother us. It's kind of like a hold-over to the Christmas Truce during World War I."

Expertly flicking cards to each of the men at the table, he grinned at their expressions of disgust. "What's the matter, boys, don't like what you're holding?"

Private Turner shook his head. "It's not just that you dealt me a rotten hand, it's that I can't for the life of me see how you did it!"

Chuckling, Carl walked away, wondering when operations would resume. He got his answer on the 5th of January, when his platoon was called into the main briefing room, along with the entire brigade. "Starting this morning, US forces began Phase I of an operation designed to clear out VC dominance in the Iron Triangle. They have assaulted Ben Suc, positioned blocking elements, and will soon be beginning deportation of the villagers from the area. Starting on the eighth, you will be linking up with elements of the 1st Infantry Division and the 11th Armored Cavalry Regiment to enter, bisect, and clear the Iron Triangle."

After going over the finer points and details, the brigade was dismissed. As they walked out, Lieutenant Daniels looked over at Lieutenant Kentworthy. "Well, it looks like we're starting to ramp up operations. Any chance we might start launching an offensive across the border any time soon?"

Lieutenant Kentworthy shrugged. "Who knows; maybe."

On the 8th of January, Phase II of Operation Cedar Falls kicked off as the 173rd Airborne Brigade, backed by elements of the 1st Infantry Division and the 11th Armored Cavalry Regiment, charged into the Iron Triangle; 155 kilometers of Viet Cong-dominated territory approximately 20 kilometers north of Saigon. Several of the more northerly search and destroy operations Lieutenant Daniels had participated in had brushed up against the border of the Iron Triangle, but he had never actually been in it. Most of the 173rd's job consisted of securing landing zones and pushing ahead of the rest of the assault force; who followed up to secure the captured territory as they cut the Iron Triangle in half. With that accomplished, they began moving to clear the Iron Triangle in a massive sweep. Trudging through the bomb-blasted and shell-shattered jungle still reeling from the massive pre-assault bombardment, Lieutenant Daniels wondered when they were going to hit their first major engagement. It had been a week and a half since they first hit boots-to-ground in the Iron Triangle, and so far their largest fight had been against twenty-odd Viet Cong who had fought for less than ten minutes before running away; the attempted pursuit had cost Third Platoon their point man, and Kit had barely avoided a set of punji pits, forcing them to slow down and losing track of their elusive enemy. Suddenly the man just ahead of him dropped to the ground as the crack of a sniper rifle resounded through the trees. Dropping to his belly, Lieutenant Daniels crawled behind the burned and shell-riven skeleton of a tree, yelling for his men to get down. "Someone find me that sniper!" hollered Private First Class Holland, finger twitching against the trigger of his M79. Pulling off his helmet, Corporal Winters placed it on a tree branch, cautiously raising it above the bush he was hiding behind. Another shot cracked through the quiet, and the helmet bounded off of the stick as a bullet smashed through it. Grabbing the helmet, Corporal Winters gave it a quick examination before rolling over to face PFC Holland, pointing at a mostly intact tree almost seventy yards ahead at a slight angle to their position. Rising to one knee behind the blackened remains of a bamboo thicket, Private First Class Holland brought the M79 to his shoulder and pulled the trigger; the grenade blasting into the base of the tree. Almost dropping the live grenade in his haste, Holland reloaded and got the next shot within two meters of the sniper's approximate position, blowing him out of the tree, along with one of the branches he had been sheltering in. Turning, he waved a hand over his head. "Clear!"

Raising a hand in acknowledgement, Platoon Sergeant Bellamy rose to his feet. "Forward!"

Lugging the dead man with them, they called in a helicopter to remove him at the next feasible landing zone; sending out three more dead and wounded in the same run. Watching the helicopter clattering off over the horizon, Lieutenant Daniels clenched his teeth in helpless anger, then forced himself to put it from his mind. You couldn't change anything about how they died; it's not like you sent them into a stupid attack, they died from the enemy. If you dwell on their deaths, you'll go mad. Moving forward, they paused at evening, the platoon leaders conferring with Captain Morgan about the night's planned activities. "All right; Lieutenant Schumacher has detailed Dog Company to move to ambush a VC encampment that reconnaissance discovered about three kilometers from our current position on a heading of West-Northwest 289°, here. First Platoon will take the sentries out, move into the camp to retrieve documents and prisoners from the command tent, and then fire a red starburst flare as the signal once they have withdrawn from the camp. On the signal, the other three platoons, which will be deployed here, here, and here, will open fire on the camp. Any questions?"

No one answered, and he nodded. "All right then. Go with God, gentlemen."

Accepting the flare gun, Lieutenant Daniels went to join the rest of his men. After lining up, they each performed the 'noise check', jumping up and down as Sergeant Bellamy walked down the line to listen for any loose gear or half-filled canteens. With a few pieces of gear secured, and two canteens refilled, they headed out, taking the heading off of a compass Lieutenant Daniels carried, and periodically checking it by the light of a shielded flashlight held under a poncho. After a tense forty-five minute walk, they made it to the Viet Cong camp. Deploying the men in a line to fire on the camp once the ambush started, Lieutenant Daniels moved to stand with Corporal Winters and Sergeant Bellamy. Looking quizzically at him, Corporal Winters spoke, his voice one step above a whisper. "Sir, what are you doing?"

His face determined, Lieutenant Daniels replied. "I'm coming with you and Roland to take out the sentries."

Corporal Winters was about to protest, when

something in Lieutenant Daniels's eyes registered, and he decided against it. Pulling a wire garrote out of his pack, he gestured for Bellamy and Daniels to follow him and flitted forward toward the perimeter. After a cautious circumnavigation of the camp, they had identified eight sentries; obviously both trying to stay alert, and tired, they were not paying as close attention to their job as they might have had they known that the enemy were less than five meters from them. Stopping by a palm tree that had been torn apart by shrapnel, Kit spoke. "All right; Roland, you take the ones on the left and the one on the far side to the left, I'll take the ones on the right and the far-side right, and you can take the two in the middle, Lieutenant."

Nodding, Lieutenant Daniels fought a mix of resentment that he had not been allotted one of the extra sentries and nervousness over what he was about to do. With a small smile that said he knew exactly what Lieutenant Daniels was thinking, Corporal Winters shook hands with both of them. "All right, then gentlemen. Good luck."

Belly-crawling forward, Lieutenant Daniels approached his first target, who was conveniently out of line-of-sight from his fellow sentry; leaning against a tree, he had his rifle loosely cradled in his arm as he rubbed at his eyes with the other. Rising behind him, Lieutenant Daniels carefully drew the knife Rhiannon had given to him; briefly pressing his lips to the engraving on the hilt, he gripped it in an 'ice-pick' hold, the blade jutting downward from the bottom of his fist with the razor-sharp edge inward. Taking a long step forward, he slapped his hand over the sentry's mouth and pulled his head back as he plunged the blade into the man's throat just above the collarbone, drawing it hard across and twisting it, clenching his eyes shut and turning his head to shield his face behind the back of his opponent's head as his hands flailed and clawed frantically, feet kicking desperately as he drowned in his own blood, finally growing still. Wiping the knife carefully on the dead man's jacket, Lieutenant Daniels took a deep breath as he mentally reconciled himself with what he had done, then began belly-crawling toward the second sentry. Less than twenty feet into his journey, the sentry came walking into his field of vision, likely going to check on the other one. Pausing within five feet of Lieutenant Daniels, he pulled out a cigarette and cupped his hand around the flame of a lighter. Breathing a silent prayer of thanks for small miracles; the flame would destroy the sentry's night vision, and his focus on the cigarette would distract him from looking around; Lieutenant Daniels rose to his feet and ran across the distance separating them, ramming the startled sentry against a tree and clamping a hand across his mouth as he stabbed him in the chest just below the sternum, twisted the blade and withdrew it, and then plunged the blade into his neck just below the collarbone, letting the sentry ease to the ground as his legs collapsed. His diaphragm destroyed by the first blow and his subclavian and brachiocephalic arteries severed along with his windpipe by the second strike, the sentry was able to offer little effectual resistance aside from a brief spasm of flailing, and quickly grew still. Dragging him further into the trees, Lieutenant Daniels cleaned and sheathed his knife, retreating to the rendezvous point Corporal Winters had designated. He did not have very long to wait before he was rejoined by Corporal Winters and Sergeant Bellamy; glancing at the blood on his hands, Corporal Winters looked up at his face. "You good, Sir?"

Nodding, Lieutenant Daniels turned back toward where they had left the rest of the platoon. "Yeah; I'm fine. Let's go."

Returning to the platoon, they quietly filtered into the sleeping camp. Leaving one or two men at each tent, they strung out along the route to the command tent, where

Sergeant Bellamy stood outside the tent while Corporal Winters and Lieutenant Daniels slipped inside to collect the prisoners and documents that awaited. Inside, they found three men asleep on blankets. Pouncing on them, they gagged and bound them, beginning the search for documents. Rifling through a bag, Lieutenant Daniels was neatly piling the contents to one side when he caught a strange look from Corporal Winters. "What are you doing, Sir?"

Lieutenant Daniels shrugged. "What does it look like I'm doing, packing for a trip to Hawaii? I'm searching for documents!"

Rolling his eyes, Corporal Winters waved a comparative hand at the difference between the neat organized piles Lieutenant Daniels was creating, and the chaos left in the wake of his own search. "I can see that, but why are you wasting time keeping things neat?"

Lieutenant Daniels looked miffed. "I believe in keeping things neat and orderly as often as possible, okay? You have a problem with that?"

Corporal Winters heaved a sigh. "Not normally, but time is kind of pressed right now, and it won't matter in the long run what shape this place is left in when we wipe it out."

Lieutenant Daniels continued his neat searching. "Well, I'm still going to search my way; I'm not criticizing your messy searching, so don't criticize my neat searching, all right?"

With a snort of exasperation, Corporal Winters broke open another box, pausing as he grappled through the contents. "Jackpot! Sir, I think we just found where these guys keep their stuff!"

Crawling over on his hands and knees from where he had been kneeling next to the box he had been searching through, Lieutenant Daniels pulled out a small flashlight, throwing a blanket over his head and the box as he examined some of the papers. With a grunt of agreement, he yanked the blanket off his head, folding it neatly and laying it to one side before assisting a muttering Corporal Winters in gathering the documents into a bag and hoisting the prisoners to their feet. Placing a knife in the first man's back, Corporal Winters prodded him toward the entrance to the tent, handing him off to Sergeant Bellamy before going back for the other one, as Lieutenant Daniels had already begun moving the last one outside. Pushing the last one out, he shoved him forward, muttering to himself. "Search neatly, leave things nicely, take your time! 'I'm not criticizing your messy searching'. What have I gotten myself into?"

Retreating out of the camp, they made their way out of the projected line of fire, then Sergeant Bellamy, who had been making a swift head count to make sure that they were all there, turned to Lieutenant Daniels. "All good, Sir."

Nodding acknowledgement, Lieutenant Daniels reached into his pack and pulled out a flare gun, sliding the round into the breech and aiming at the sky. As he pulled the trigger, a small red light arced upward like a homesick meteor before exploding into a starburst of colored light. As he began packing the flare gun away, Sergeant Bellamy was already getting the platoon into motion. "Charlie can see where dat flare came from, Sir, and if he's in the area, he'll be coming down on us. We gotta move."

Amid the sudden cascade of fury as three platoons poured their fire into the camp; with M16 rifles, M60 machine guns, M79 grenade launchers, M2 mortars, and M72 LAW rocket launchers hammering their hate into the flimsy shelters and unarmored tents; First Platoon ran through the pitch-black, enveloping darkness of a jungle night, making their way around the encampment and back toward the rest of the company. As the the fire lashing the camp ceased, they angled back toward the line, bypassing Fourth Platoon and moving to intersect with Third. As they got closer, they could hear Captain Morgan speaking to Lieutenant Kentworthy. "Good work so far, Lieutenant. Now as soon as First gets back, we'll know what kind of results we got out of this."

Lieutenant Kentworthy was about to reply when Platoon Sergeant Piper suddenly clicked on his flashlight, illuminating the men of First Platoon less than thirty yards away. "Looks like most of 'em got back all right, Sir; and if I'm not mistaken, they've got some prisoners."

Hoisting a hurried salute, having handed his prisoner off to one of the other men, Lieutenant Daniels motioned to the prisoners, as well as the bag that 'Surfer' carried. "Yes Sir, we do; also we managed to get some maps and dispatches; from the look of them, they contain intelligence about Viet Cong movements in the Iron Triangle."

Returning the salute, Captain Morgan turned to his radio operator. "All right; notify Lieutenant Colonel Schumacher that the raid was a success, and then have the rest of the company get moving back to camp. Well done, gentlemen."

As they prepared to bivouac for the night, Corporal Winters stopped by Lieutenant Daniels's tent. "So; you've killed men with your rifle, you've led a night raid on an enemy camp, killed two men with a knife, and gone into the enemy's camp to take prisoners and intelligence. Feeling like you're pretty bad stuff, huh?"

Lieutenant Daniels looked uncomfortable. "I don't exactly know, Corporal. When I felt that guy's life leave him, I wanted to throw up. When we were walking into the camp, I wanted to wet my pants. So, no, I don't feel like particularly bad stuff; I just want to keep my men alive."

With an understanding nod, Corporal Winters clapped a hand on his shoulder. "Well, Sir, I understand you don't like it, but I think you have the gift in you; a bit of the innate ability to perform these kinds of tasks. It can be trained, but some people have it naturally; given the amount of training and experience you've had, and how you handled tonight's mission, I would put money on you being the latter."

As he turned away, Lieutenant Daniels snorted. "Corporal, you'd put money on whether I was going to sneeze in my sleep or not."

Corporal Winters hesitated for just the barest instant, something flickering deep in his eyes, then he turned back, a whimsical smile on his face. "Do you sneeze in your sleep? Care to put some odds up?"

Blissfully unaware of what had just happened, Lieutenant Daniels rolled his eyes. "Yechh! I don't know if that's even a thing; I just said that out of the top of my head."

A light grin concealing what was going on behind his amused expression, Corporal Winters nodded agreement. "I jest, Lieutenant, I jest."

With a swift salute, he turned away, eyes dark with anger and nostrils flaring with the release of his concealed emotions as he made his way back to his tent. Reaching into his jacket pocket, he pulled out a creased, dirty envelope, removing the sweat-stained paper inside with shaking hands as he held it up to the light of the full moon, re-reading the crisp, emotionless words that had already burned their way into his tortured mind and broken heart.

Dear Kit,

I am writing you to inform you that I have successfully filed for divorce; this is our last communication, as I can no longer maritally associate myself with someone who would willingly join a fight America has no business entering in the first place. If you attempt to contact me after this letter, I will take legal action against you.

Lila.

Two tears tracking their way down his cheek, Kit re-folded the letter and pressed his lips agains the folded paper, sliding the letter back into the envelope in the now-familiar nightly ritual he had begun since receiving the letter. "Good night, Lila. May you find happiness with your new life," he whispered, before placing the envelope back into his jacket and rolling up in his blanket, his thoughts turning to what the Lieutenant had said. In truth, he would not have placed money on that ridiculous idea; but the fights in Saigon provided an outlet for his grief and frustrated anger. The thrill of gambling with something other than his heart helped at least temporarily salve the wound, and he mentally pictured himself in the ring against whatever had turned his wife against him on occasion; the times when his fighter won gave him brief satisfaction over his anger, while the times when his fighter lost he simply wrote off as an acceptable loss and an enjoyable reprieve.

The morning dawned grey and overcast, with drizzling rain threatening to become more serious as the day wore on. Continuing their advance, the platoon encountered little resistance until midmorning, when a patrol of about fifteen Viet Cong ambushed them. Fortunately, one of the enemy riflemen showed himself about forty feet too early, giving them time to react and engage, whereupon the enemy scattered into the jungle; pursuing, the platoon was just close enough to see one of them dropping into the ground. Skidding to a baffled halt, Corporal Winters and Lance Corporal Masters, who had been leading the pursuit, looked at each other before glancing back at Sergeant Bellamy and Lieutenant Daniels, who had been hotfooting it behind them with the radio operator panting in their wake. "Um, looks like we just hit some of the tunnel networks they warned us about."

Nodding, Lieutenant Daniels grabbed the handset

as the radio operator wiped sweat and rain from his face, tilting his canteen and taking a long drink. "Dog Six, Dog Six, this is Dog One Six; I am at Romeo Whiskey, Zero-Two-Four, Zero-Five-Nine Zero-Four-Three degrees, requesting tunnel clearing operators, over."

"Roger that, Dog One Six, tunnel rats are inbound, out."

A few minutes later, a quartet of small, skinny soldiers came walking up to the platoon, who were standing around the tunnel entrance. "This the tunnel, Sir?"

As Lieutenant Daniels nodded, the leader of the group grabbed a pair of satchel charges and slung them on, checking the loads in his suppressed .38 revolver and clicking his flashlight on. "Wish me luck."

One by one they dropped into the tunnel, vanishing into the darkness. Lieutenant Daniels had expected to wait until they had cleared and destroyed the tunnel, and was startled when Sergeant Bellamy began preparing the men to move out. "Sergeant, aren't we supposed to act as the security element for the tunnel rats?"

Shaking his head, Bellamy motioned for Corporal Winters to start moving. "No, Sir. De First infantry gonna be coverin' de tunnel rats; we gotta be movin' on and clearin' out de Triangle. 'Toon move out!"

The entire company received no further enemy contact for the rest of the day, although Alpha and Charlie Companies reported light casualties from booby traps and brief firefights with the retreating enemy. Intelligence was suggesting that many of the predicted numbers of enemy were escaping across the border into Cambodia, and so the 173rd was ordered to push faster in an effort to catch up to them. Kills mounted slightly over the next week as they caught up to a group of Viet Cong fighters, but overall, they found very few actual enemy soldiers. As they were reaching the edge of the Iron Triangle, Lieutenant Daniels spotted a Vietnamese woman running towards the edge of the clearing they were crossing. As he was about to call out to her, a rifle shot cracked in the warm, slightly humid air; now comparatively cooler and drier than when he had arrived. A spurt of earth kicked skyward less than a foot from her, and as she jinked away from it, fumbling with something in her hands, two more bullets caught her in the back, knocking her to the ground. Face reddening with shocked anger, Lieutenant Daniels turned to Sergeant Piper, who had fired the shots. "Sergeant! What in Heaven's name do you think you're doing? That woman was an unarmed civilian, and you just shot her down in cold blood! As soon as we get back to base, I'm going to have you court-martialed!"

Running forward, he knelt beside the woman's body, turning her over. His breath caught in his throat as he saw what she had in her hands; a battered and rusty, but still functional-looking French-made MAT 49 submachine gun.Looking up with horrified eyes at Sergeant Piper and Lieutenant Kentworthy, who had joined him at the body, Lieutenant Daniels swallowed twice before he was able to speak. "I-I'm sorry, Sergeant; I had no idea; I thought-"

He was unable to finish the thought, gesturing mutely at the woman's body. Nodding grimly, Sergeant Piper lit a fresh cigar off of the butt of his old one. "Yep. That's what one of the men in my platoon thought about three weeks before you got here. He saw a teenaged girl with a basket, and didn't think of checking what was in the basket, and he got himself and four of his buddies killed when the girl popped a potato-masher grenade out of the basket and chucked it at 'em. That woman was probably gonna scoot into the brush and ambush us or else spread the word that we were here and grab some of her fellow guerrillas and pop an ambush on our heads."

He shrugged. "It's not your fault you didn't see it, Sir. It's pure luck I saw it myself."

Pulling the pin on a grenade, he carefully wedged it under her torso so that raising or turning her body over would arm the grenade. Catching a disapproving look from Lieutenant Daniels, he shrugged again. "What? The Cong lay booby traps, and they try to get their dead out of here when they can, so who says I can't lay a surprise for anyone who comes back for her?"

Lieutenant Daniels still looked disapproving. "What if an innocent civilian family member comes back for her, or American troops?"

Lieutenant Kentworthy broke in as they reformed the skirmish line, beginning to move forward again. "Both of those are unlikely; the first option because this whole area has been declared a free-fire zone, and anybody in this area is automatically suspected of being/classified as a Viet Cong guerrilla; that's one of the reasons Sergeant Piper was watching for weapons more closely when that woman broke cover. The second option is unlikely because we are going to be pulling out of the Iron Triangle as soon as we finish clearing it."

Lieutenant Daniels grunted. "More of the 'war of attrition, hold on until they cry Uncle, don't hold any ground because it might provoke Russia and China' banana oil?"

As Lieutenant Kentworthy and Sergeant Piper nodded, he continued. "Okay, I'll buy that, but what if scavengers get to her before her buddies do?"

Sergeant Piper looked indifferent. "I don't like scavengers either."

The remainder of the offensive passed relatively uneventfully: a double-dozen booby traps that killed or incapacitated fifteen men of Dog Company including two of Lieutenant Daniels's men, two snipers that claimed the lives of three of Lieutenant Seybold's platoon, and a pair of ambushes; one initiated by the enemy which claimed Fourth Platoon's point man and Lieutenant Kentworthy's primary M79 gunner; the other initiated by Dog Company which killed thirteen enemy fighters. As Operation Cedar Falls was winding down, the 173rd was pulled out to prepare for another operation being prepared to hit the mobile, and frustratingly elusive, Central Office of South Vietnam; the Communist 'headquarters' of the uprising. In what was becoming a familiar 'hammer and anvil' tactic, the 173rd would be dropped in on one side of the territory to be engaged, and they would then form the 'anvil' for the enemy to be crushed against by the 'hammer' which consisted of substantial elements of the 1st and 25th Infantry Divisions, and the 11th Armored Cavalry Regiment. Packing his gear for the mission, Lieutenant Daniels pondered the ramifications of their insertion. At the briefing, they had been told the 2nd Battalion would be parachuting in, while they would be airlifted in by helicopter along with 4th Battalion and the 196th Light Infantry. As he was finishing packing and adjusting his gear to prep for the mission, the battalion chaplain approached. "Lieutenant, as we prepare to go into battle, I am going to be holding a brief service for the men, and I was wondering if you would release your platoon to join me if they so desire."

Nodding, Lieutenant Daniels relinquished his grip on the straps to his pack. "Gladly; and I would not mind attending myself."

Quickly walking over to where the rest of the men were putting the finishing touches on their packing, the chaplain cleared his throat to gain their attention. "Men, as we are preparing to go into battle, I am going to be holding a brief service, if you wish to join me."

Sergeant Bellamy, a devout Catholic, nodded quickly, moving to join the chaplain, followed by Corporal Winters and Lance Corporal Masters, 'Surfer', PFC Holland, and Private Turner. Most of the other men, however, declined; Lieutenant Daniels's presence, and the knowledge that he had chosen to join the chaplain's service kept them at least verbally respectful in their rejection of the offer, but several of them were clearly only keeping it nice because of Lieutenant Daniels. Clenching his teeth, he took a hissing breath, biting his tongue hard to forestall the acid comments he wanted to bestow upon them, and turned to follow the chaplain to the area he was conducting the service. Kneeling near the back as the chaplain began to speak, he was startled to see Lieutenant Kentworthy two rows ahead of him, along with the grim, taciturn Sergeant Piper. Huh. I guess I could have seen that Mark was a Christian, but I didn't exactly see Piper as a Christian. You learn something new everyday.

The chaplain's voice broke him from his thoughts. "Let us bow our heads and pray."

Bowing his head, he offered up a heartfelt prayer for his men, for their safety, and for Rhiannon, waiting at home for him. Raising a hand over the assembled men, the chaplain spoke, his resonant voice rolling out over their bowed heads. "Almighty God, we come before you this day, lifting our hearts to you. As we prepare ourselves to enter the Valley of Death, we ask that you would walk beside us; guarding and guiding us with Thy rod and Thy staff, to comfort us and to protect us. May we ever remember that it is to You that the glory belongs, for Thine is the Kingdom, the Power, and the Glory forever. In the name of Your Son we pray, Amen."

As a chorus of 'Amens' rose from the men, the chaplain concluded. "May His Peace fill you, may His Presence cover you, may His Hand protect you, and may His Arm guide you. Go with God."

Rising to his feet, Lieutenant Daniels shook hands with his men as they returned to the assembly area. "Good luck, gentlemen."

One of the men who had declined to attend the

service walked over to Lieutenant Daniels, his body language indicating he was either struggling for words or else choosing them carefully. "Lieutenant, I don't mean to be rude, but why exactly do you attend the services the chaplain offers? I mean, what's the point? Is praying and reciting Bible verses going to stop you from getting killed out there? Will it stop a bullet, or keep a mine from going off if you step on it? Is God going to magically make your helicopter not crash, or stuff like that?"

Lieutenant Daniels paused as he pondered the question. "Well, I don't think that He's going to magically stop me from getting shot if that's not in His plan, but I do believe that he will keep me safe if that's his plan; and if it's not, well, then I'm going to die. That's not to say that I'm going to do something stupid because I believe that I'm going to die if it's my time and I'm not if it's not, because that would be putting God to the test; and that's something that's strictly forbidden in the Bible, so I really don't want to do that, but for me at least, prayer and services before battle help me center myself, make peace with the idea of dying, and remind myself where I'm going if I should be so unfortunate as to die; kind of a way to prepare for what's coming in a spiritual and mental sense more than any kind of real physical sense."

Rubbing his chin, the man considered that for a moment, then nodded. "Okay, well, good for you, Sir. Hope it helps you out."

Nodding as the man turned back to his gear, Lieutenant Daniels gave a small smile. "Yes, it does."

Finally the brigade was ready to go, and they began boarding the helicopters that would take them to the Landing Zones. Following the usual procedures, they dashed into a defensive perimeter around the Landing Zone as the M60 gunners on the helicopters hosed the area with fire, then regrouped and prepared to move out. Hiking across a belt of grasslands, Dog Company entered their defensive positions, digging in and preparing to await the enemy who would hopefully be pushed into them by the advancing 11th Armored Cavalry Regiment, 1st Infantry Division, and 25th Infantry Division. The first few days were fairly quiet, and as he was conducting a perimeter check on his platoon, which bordered the entrenchments of Third Platoon, he heard a familiar voice in the noonday stillness. "Check."

Brow furrowing in puzzlement, he jogged over to the foxhole from whence the voice had come, staring down at Sergeant Lyman and Corporal Hanson from Third Platoon, who were sitting in the bottom of the hole across a chess board from each other. Looking up as Lieutenant Daniels's boot accidentally kicked a small shower of dirt onto his leg, Sergeant Lyman shaded his eyes against the glare of the sun, teeth flashing in a grin of recognition. "Good afternoon, Sir! I was wondering if you were going to come around at some point; but I didn't expect you until later. Corporal Hanson is a pretty good chess player in his own right, and we decided to settle once and for all who's better."

Lieutenant Daniels was about to reprimand the grinning Sergeant for failing to watch his assigned sector, when he noticed Corporal Winters belly-down about twenty feet away, a pair of hooded binoculars in his grip as he glassed the tree-line on the far side of the plain, and swallowed his words unspoken, instead crouching on the edge of the foxhole and eyeing the board. "How do you propose to do that?"

Sergeant Lyman indicated a cardboard supply box that had been ripped in half to provide a flat surface, and a pen sitting next to the cardboard on which a pair of initials had been scrawled, with a line marking a barrier between them. "Simple. The same way they do at the chess championships internationally. First player to win six games wins the title of champion."

With a slightly sardonic smirk, Lieutenant Daniels jerked his chin in Corporal Winters's direction. "You get Kit to put up any odds as to who's going to win?"

Sergeant Lyman shook his head. "We offered him the chance when we asked him to spot for us, but he wasn't having any of it."

Lieutenant Daniels considered this for a moment, then shrugged. "Huh. Well, who's winning so far?"

The two men looked at each other for a moment, then back at Lieutenant Daniels. Sergeant Lyman was the first to break the silence. "Well, so far, we've only played two games, and both of them were stalemated, so; nobody is."

Nodding, Lieutenant Daniels rose to his feet. "Okay. Not to put loyalty to my teammates first or anything like that, but if I were a betting man my money would be on Jimmy. Make sure you keep at least one eye out; and don't let Sergeant Bellamy or Sergeant Piper catch you doing this; for that matter, it would probably be a bad idea to let Captain Morgan catch you, either. Good luck gentlemen."

Exchanging salutes, he moved on down the perimeter. They were not expecting enemy contact for at least a few more days; reports indicated that the enemy was choosing to stand and fight thus far; the cynics theorized that they were trying to buy their headquarters time to get away, but nobody in High Command wanted to believe that they had anywhere to go but through the 173rd and 196th, so they had been dug in and constructed fortified positions to prevent any retreat by the expected enemy. It was nearly three weeks before they received any kind of enemy contact; but on the morning of the 18th of March the sentries reported enemy contact to the position's front. Grabbing his helmet and clamping it on his head as Private Turner roused him, Lieutenant Daniels raced to the front line, raising his binoculars to scan the tree line. Sure enough, he could make out black-clad figures moving about in the trees and long grass. Grabbing the radio, he called Captain Morgan. "Dog Six, Dog Six, this is Dog One Six, I make approximately two hundred gooks in the tree line; no sign of heavy equipment, looks like Charlie decided to pay us a visit, over."

"Roger that, Dog One Six, I'll see what kind of air assets we have in the area; Dog Six out."

Moving at a dead run to where Lance Corporal Masters was positioned on the platoon's flank, Lieutenant Daniels checked to make sure that he had plenty of ammunition, then turned as Sergeant Bellamy came running up. "Just checked with de mortar team, dey good to go. Just waiting for Charlie to come out and fight."

Nodding his thanks, Lieutenant Daniels followed him back to a larger foxhole slightly back from the line, but still close enough that he could move and communicate along the line. In the hole was a radio to communicate back to Battalion Headquarters, as well as both Lieutenant Kentworthy and Sergeant Piper, who had also been called to action when the sentry's call came through. "Morning Lieutenant; morning Sergeant. Fancy some action?"

Returning Sergeant Piper's salute, and exchanging salutes with Lieutenant Kentworthy, Lieutenant Daniels shrugged. "I guess so. I mean, it makes a change from being bored out of my skull, but I'd rather be bored out of my skull than have my or my soldiers's brains blown out of their skulls. Still, if they're coming this way, maybe they'll be moving the headquarters everyone's talking about this way soon, and we can pin 'em down so that the Air Force, or artillery, or somebody can roll them under or bomb them out of existence or some such thing."

Lieutenant Kentworthy nodded absently, his gaze fixed on the enemy position, which was becoming more and more active; clearly preparing for an assault. "Yeah;

that would be nice."

Sensing something in his tone, Lieutenant Daniels turned to look at him. "What; you don't think they're coming?"

Lieutenant Kentworthy grimaced. "Call me cynical, or doom-sayer, or whatever you want to, but I'm of the opinion that their 'headquarters' is already safe and sound across the border in Cambodia, and that this whole operation was compromised before it even got off the ground. That said, I'm willing to hold out a faint hope that maybe, just maybe, there's something out there that might be the headquarter's we're looking for, and that even if there isn't, that smashing up this group of NVA soldiers and Viet Cong irregulars will bloody Hanoi's nose badly enough that they think twice before trying to dominate any major area of South Vietnam again, and that this victory will give us enough positive balance, or morale points, or whatever you want to call it, with the South Vietnamese Army and the American High Command, that they finally give us the go-ahead to cross the border, chase the VC and NVA right back up the Ho Chi Minh Trail all the way to Hanoi, and raise the American and South Vietnamese flags in Hanoi; but I really don't think that any of that is going to happen, and that whatever does get reported of this battle will paint it as a failure to the American public."

As Lieutenant Daniels cast a shocked look in his direction, he nodded. "I know, I know, it's not a very nice thought, but from a couple of letters I've gotten from home, the press isn't being very supportive of what's going on here in what little coverage they're giving us, and it's getting worse."

Lieutenant Daniels was about to reply when a mortar shell suddenly ripped the ground thirty yards away, showering the hole and its occupants with dirt and debris as they dived for the bottom of the hole. Rifle and machine gun fire crackled and chattered from the woods, and Viet Cong guerrillas began to advance across the fifty or so yards of open ground towards the American position. Instant return fire blazed from the American lines as the platoon gunners opened up, along with a section of 81mm mortars set up further back. A carefully called in air strike destroyed the VC mortars with machine gun fire and bombs, and the American mortars began marching along the tree line, hunting the machine guns hidden therein. In their foxhole, Lieutenant Daniels checked the map, turning to Lieutenant Kentworthy. "Okay, the mortars are down; I'm going forward to check on the men."

Climbing out of the hole with Sergeant Bellamy and his radio operator in tow, he moved at a crouching run across the twenty or so yards between his hole and the foxholes of First Platoon. "Sound off!"

As he half-crawled, half-ran behind and between the line of holes, he felt a wave of relief as each of his men responded with affirmative calls. "All right, direct your fire at the flank; we've still got some machine guns on that sector!"

Dashing back to where the command foxhole was dug, he dropped in, ducking as a hail of bullets hummed threateningly by overhead. Grabbing the radio, he rolled to the radio channel between himself and the platoon mortar team. "All right, direct your fire ten 'o clock, your position, three hundred, three hundred twenty yards!"

As affirmative replies crackled back through the radio, and 60mm shells began to crash down on the area indicated, the enemy assault began to crumble, then fall back, the survivors running for the shelter of the trees. As they ran, 'Surfer' jumped up in his hole, shaking his rifle over his head in victory. "Ha, that'll teach you to mess with the 173rd, you little maggots!"

"Surfer, get down!" Shouted Lieutenant Daniels as he

exploded up out of his foxhole, racing across the intervening distance and diving squarely into the young man's back, tackling him to the bottom of the foxhole. As they collided, he felt a sudden impact from the other side of his target's body, and something splashed on his cheek: warm and sticky, with a coppery smell that raised the hairs on the back of his neck. Picking himself up, he rolled 'Surfer' over, his worst fears confirmed as he spotted the bullet wound in his upper chest; a through-and-through that had sprayed the blood that now covered Lieutenant Daniels's cheek and neck. Face contorted in surprise and pain, 'Surfer' clutched at the wound, blood running in a trickle of scarlet from his mouth. Fighting to speak around the blood in his mouth, he failed, more blood running from his nose as he did so. Half-rising from his knees, Lieutenant Daniels poked his head over the lip of the foxhole, looking around. "MEDIC! MEDIC! MEDIC!"

Returning his attention to the dying infantryman on the floor of the foxhole next to him; sparing a brief glance for his foxhole mate who had already been shot and killed, Lieutenant Daniels pressed a bandage from his first-aid kit to the wound, baring his teeth as the bandage soaked through almost before he had begun applying it. "Hang on, Private; Doc's almost here. Hang in there; that's an order!"

Dropping into the hole with a thud, the heavyset medic unceremoniously shoved Lieutenant Daniels to the side, hands busy with shears and gauze, tape and a large-bore needle as he sealed off the entrance and exit wounds and inserted the needle between the ribs just below the collarbone to remove air from the chest cavity. That done, he waved to the stretcher bearers who had come at a run when the call went out for a medic. "All right, this guy's priority; move it!"

As they were lifting him out of the foxhole and onto the stretcher, he gave an encouraging smile, clasping

'Surfer' on the shoulder. "Looks like you got your ticket home, son."

On his other side, Lieutenant Daniels grabbed his hand. "Good luck, Surfer. Safe travels."

Barely conscious as they inserted an IV drip, 'Surfer' did not acknowledge either man, his eyes closed as his head lolled to one side. Turning away as the stretcher was rushed towards the descending helicopter, the medic let his smile slip, revealing a face hollowed by stress and anxiety as he wiped the blood off of his hands with a cloth he had dampened from his canteen. "It's not good, Lieutenant. The bullet looks like it clipped his spine, and he's lost a lot of blood. I can't deal with the internal bleeding, and he's got a lot of that, from the looks of things; plus, it appears that he is aspirating some blood, which means probable lung compromise."

Lieutenant Daniels ground his teeth. "Just give me the end of this, Doc. Will he live?"

Scrubbing his hands across his face, the medic glared at an unoffending lizard that skittered past. "I can't say for certain."

Lieutenant Daniels stifled a growl of impatience. "But?"

Transferring his glare of frustration and helpless fury to a rock as the lizard scuttled out of sight, the medic hurled the balled-up cloth away from himself as if it burned him. "But I don't think he's going to make it, Sir. I'm sorry. Really I am; but that bullet bounced around some before coming out his back, and it did a lot of internal damage."

Squeezing his eyes shut, Lieutenant Daniels pressed his clenched fist to his mouth as he fought to control the anger and sorrow coursing through him. "Thanks for letting me know, Doc. Sorry I couldn't get there sooner."

Shaking his head with an angry gesture of denial, the medic turned away, his attention already focused on the other wounded they had sustained during the fight.

While the other battalions reported moderate contact with the enemy over the next few days, 1/503 was not engaged further, and soon received word that they would be being pulled out. It turned out that on the morning they were attacked, the second phase of the operation had kicked off; with an extensive push being conducted from west to east across Tay Ninh Province, the need for 'Anvil Force' was no longer in existence. Returning to Bien Hoa airbase, they conducted one or two search and destroy patrols, but turned up little activity. Mail had stacked up, and Lieutenant Daniels found two or three letters from Rhiannon waiting for him when he returned. They mostly concerned mundane, ordinary things, like her job at the library, how she had gotten a cat named Darryl who had a very opinion of himself and a commensurately low opinion of the neighbor's dog, and that she had begun cultivating a cactus. This last revelation came as something of a shock to Lieutenant Daniels, but as she explained in the letter,

I know this may seem weird, but growing a cactus is an ideal choice for the climate around here, and it doesn't require a lot of care, so if I forget to water it regularly it's not a big problem. My only problem is that Darryl keeps trying to use it as a scratching post, with predictable results, so we go around and around on that particular battle, with me trying to stop him and him trying to overcome whatever barricades I construct.

Imagining Rhiannon squaring off with a big calico tomcat, placing various kinds of fencing around her beloved cactus plant, while the cat squalled complaints about the needles in its paws but kept stubbornly coming back for more, Carl smiled. His smile dimmed as he remembered the news he had received on the battalion's return to the airbase. Despite the doctor's best efforts, Private Ken Barkley, also known as 'Surfer', had bled to death from the internal injuries he had sustained on the battle line during the defense of 1/503's position. His was not the only loss, but it was by far the most personal for Lieutenant Daniels, given the manner of his injury and subsequent passing. Things were fairly quiet for the rest of March and April, but during the second week of May, 1/503 was given marching orders to report to the Ia Drang valley for operations against hostile elements conducting guerrilla operations against the nearby garrisons. Airlifted in to the valley, they spent less than three weeks patrolling and clashing with the enemy forces in the area before being airlifted once again, this time to the Dak To Airbase to reinforce the 4th Infantry Division.

Exchanging salutes with Brigadier General Deane, Colonel William Livsey, the Operations Officer to Major General Peers, felt a quiet sense of relief, mingled with worry. He was extremely glad that the General's request for reinforcements had been answered, and the reputation of the 'Flying Soldiers', as the men of the 173rd had come to be known in the wake of Operation Junction City, was formidable, but it was that very reputation that worried him. They knew they were the best, but thus far their only major experience in the war to date had been against People's Liberation Armed Forces, or PLAF, irregulars; guerrillas, with bad equipment and worse training more often than not. The Central Highlands were largely home to People's Army of Vietnam, or PAVN, regulars: essentially the standing army of North Vietnam, sent down via the Ho Chi Minh Trail to infiltrate South Vietnam and attack the

American and Army of the Republic of Vietnam, or ARVN, forces; well trained and equipped, they were a force to be reckoned with, but the men of the 173rd seemed to think they were pretty much invincible. Hiding his unease behind a friendly smile, he waved them to seats. "Good to meet you, gentlemen. I'm Colonel Livsey. For starters, I'd like to welcome you to Dak To Airbase. We have been experiencing a spike in enemy operations, but revised tactics are helping to reduce casualties. With that said, I would also like to caution you all that the PAVN we are up against here in the Highlands are significantly better trained, equipped, and motivated than the PLAF guerrillas. I would urge you in the strongest possible terms not to underestimate them, and to use Major General Peers's guidelines regarding unit deployment as well."

Lieutenant Colonel Schumacher spoke up. "What guidelines are those, Colonel?"

Mentally crossing his fingers that they would take him seriously, Colonel Livsey replied, "Well, for starters, battalions move as a unit out in the field; if at all possible, they don't split down further than that. If individual companies have to break off, they don't go further than one kilometer or an hours march, whichever is closer, from each other. If a unit is engaged, an immediate attempt to reinforce it is made."

He paused to look at each of them in turn, then continued. "I know this sounds a bit excessive, but please believe me when I say it's not. These guys out there are regular army soldiers, not just a bunch of guerrillas. Not to make you feel like I'm insulting your capabilities, but they have a much higher level of training and gear than the guys you've been facing up until now."

Watching their reactions, he felt his heart sink. They were being polite and quiet, but he could tell that they were not really taking him seriously. As the meeting broke up, he stared unseeingly at his desk, hoping that they would see reason before it was too late, and the lesson was learned the hard way; by blood and fire.

Lieutenant Daniels looked up at the sky, wondering if it would rain. It was November, and the temperatures were cooling off once again after the torrid temperatures of the summer months, but with that came an increase in precipitation, with rain falling for almost a third of the month of November on average. It had been fairly quiet for the men of 1/503, but the same could not be said for the rest of the brigade. Less than a week after they arrived, C Company, 2nd Battalion, had been on patrol with A Company supporting, and had discovered the bodies of a Civilian Irregular Defense Group that had been missing on the nearby hills. The next morning, A Company had been ambushed by a large force of PAVN soldiers and massacred, with over half of the Company being killed and almost half the remainder wounded. Body counts varied depending on who was asked, but it was obvious that they probably hadn't gotten as many as the newspapers said they had; or even as many as the 173rd had lost. The men of the 173rd were boiling mad about this, and the fact that additional forces were moved into the area in the aftermath didn't help their tempers. The 4th Battalion was ambushed about two weeks later, with twenty-two killed and sixty-two wounded, for three dead PAVN soldiers found in the morning after the night-long battle. In August, the ARVN 42nd Infantry Regiment, along with the ARVN 8th Airborne and Army advisors, had occupied a camp at Dad Seang, a hilltop outpost astride the Ho Chi Minh Trail, and quickly became embroiled in a vicious three-day battle that cost both sides heavily, leading the PAVN to withdraw across the border and the ARVN Airborne to withdraw to Saigon for refitting. In the aftermath of the battle, Brigadier General Deane turned over command of the 173rd to Brigadier General Leo Schweiter, and three weeks later, 1/503 received orders to protect the rice harvest in Phu Yen Province; the only real action they had had all summer. By November, however, they were being airlifted back to Dak To, as intelligence had reported the increased movement of hostile forces into the region, and the 173rd was being used to bolster defenses at Ben Het, eighteen kilometers to the east of Dak To. Today, they would be moving out in a search for the headquarters of the 66th PAVN Regiment, believed to be in a valley to the south. Checking to make sure that his canteen was full, and he had remembered to safety his M16, he walked over to join the rest of the platoon, who were lining up with Dog Company and 1/503. With the brigade assembled, they began combing the hills leading to the valley. Around noon, just as Lieutenant Daniels was beginning to think nothing was going to happen, Lieutenant Seybold's platoon ran into an enemy defensive position about thirty yards in front of him; machine guns and rockets hammering at the platoon. Dropping to the ground, Lieutenant Daniels began directing fire against the bunkers and trenches in front of them, moving to section his platoon in between Lieutenant Seybold's platoon, and Lieutenant Kentworthy's platoon, which was positioned slightly to the left and behind his current position, forming an oblique line to take the enemy position in the flank. Pouring fire into the enemy position, they waited out an artillery strike, and then advanced, forcing the enemy from the fort. Miraculously, no one from Dog Company was killed, but Captain McElwain's Charlie Company had suffered two killed and three wounded. The next few days followed a similar pattern: Patrol until they encountered an entrenched PAVN position, pin it down with suppressive fire, and call in an artillery or air strike before advancing into the ruins. As they moved further in, however, their artillery support was being stretched to the limit, so 4/503 was sent to occupy a nearby landmass known as Hill 823 to facilitate the construction of Fire Base 15. As they waited for news of the assault's outcome, Lieutenant Daniels had his men take defensive positions and dig in for the night. Walking around the perimeter to check the positioning and alertness of the sentries, he was startled to find that Kit was not alone at his post; one eye on the perimeter, he was conversing in a low voice with a man dressed in unfamiliar jungle fatigues, a bandanna wrapped around his head as he cradled an M4 carbine in his arm, danger radiating from him like smoke from a fire. Turning as Daniels stepped on a rock, his boot scraping quietly in the darkness, the stranger had a bead on him before he could blink, eyes glowing a ghostly white in the semidarkness; his face had been covered in streaks and shadows of paint that mottled his features into a blur of green and black. Almost as quickly, Corporal Winters recognized the gaping Lieutenant, and placed a firm hand on his companion's rifle barrel, pointing it at the ground. "Easy, Sir. This is Lieutenant Daniels; the one I was telling you about."

The white eyes rolled from Lieutenant Daniels to Corporal Winters and back again, then the man relaxed, extending a hand. "Sorry about that, Sir; you just startled me, is all. I didn't expect you along until a little later."

Lieutenant Daniels shook hands, feeling the power in the man's grip as he shot a look at Corporal Winters. "That happens to me a lot. Listen, Corporal, I don't mean to interrupt whatever it is you're doing here, but you do realize you're on sentry duty out here, right?"

Looking slightly sheepish, Corporal Winters nodded, gesturing at the other man. "Yes, Sir, but Petty Officer Reese here has been trying to talk to me about the transfer option for six weeks now, and our paths just crossed tonight because he moved his unit nearly twenty kilometers off of their original vector to intercept us. Frankly, Sir, Petty Officer Reese and his associates have been trying to get to talk to several of us from Dog Company for some time now; but they lost track of us when we hightailed it for Phu Yen."

Lieutenant Daniels felt the hair rise on the back of his neck as several more men, dressed in uniforms lacking any and all insignias, began making their way out of the tall grass twenty yards out from the line. Raising a hand in a halting gesture as he reached for his rifle, Petty Officer Reese shook his head. "Don't! They're not gooks; they're Hatchet Force members!"

Nodding, the gaunt, dark-haired man at the head of the group extended his hand. "Exactly. Lieutenant Daniels? Good to finally meet you."

Shaking hands again, Lieutenant Daniels bit back the urge to ask about their names; obviously they were not at liberty to say, and would probably not even give their real names if pressed. "Thanks; I think. What did you want to talk to me about?"

Teeth flashed in the gathering darkness as the man grinned. "Well, not just you, Lieutenant, but actually several of your men, and the men of Dog Company. Are they available at the moment?"

Eyes narrowing, Lieutenant Daniels shrugged. "I dunno. First tell me who you're looking for, and I'll see if I can round them up."

Nodding briskly, the man swatted at a mosquito. "Yes, of course. If you could find for me Lance Corporal Masters, Platoon Sergeant Bellamy, Lieutenant Kentworthy of Third Platoon, and Platoon Sergeant Piper and Sergeant First Class Lyman, also of Third Platoon."

His eyebrows shooting skyward, Lieutenant Daniels fought the urge to gape. "I know which platoon they're from already, but how do you know all that?"

Once again, the teeth flashed against darkly tanned skin as the stranger grinned. There was something of a wolf in that grin, Lieutenant Daniels reflected. "Let's just say I have my ways, Lieutenant. Can you get me those men in Captain Morgan's command tent in, say, fifteen minutes?"

Fighting a surge of shock at the man's knowledge of his unit's command structure, Lieutenant Daniels nodded. "Yeah, I'll see what I can do."

He turned away, then turned back, a slightly smug smirk on his face as he dropped his trump card. "I'll send someone to replace Corporal Winters as soon as I can."

If he had expected some kind of surprise or questioning on the man's face, he was disappointed; the man merely nodded. "Thank you, Lieutenant. You're right, I did want him as well."

Hiding his disappointment, Lieutenant Daniels found Private First Class Holland sitting in his foxhole, playing cards with Privates Turner and Mansfield. "You three, I need one of you to cover for Corporal Winters on sentry duty, and the other two to cover for some of the other guys."

Amid grimaces and gripes, the men climbed out of the hole, Private Turner trudging bad-temperedly toward Corporal Winters's position while the other two followed Lieutenant Daniels as he tramped through the camp, muttering to each other behind his back. Finding the men whom he sought gathered at the mess tent, he turned to the men with him. "All right, men, you can go."

The two men looked at each other, then Private First Class Holland spoke up. "Um, Sir, if you don't mind, what's going on that had you pull us out of our hole and follow you around the camp, find a couple of our teammates, and then tell us to go back to our hole?"

Weighing the request against his instinctive desire to conceal the presence of the men in the camp, Lieutenant Daniels finally shook his head. "I'm sorry, Private. I really wish I could tell you what's going on, but I can't."

Private First Class Holland looked crestfallen, but appeared to accept the response. Private Mansfield was about to protest, but Lieutenant Daniels cut him off, his voice becoming clipped. "That is all, gentlemen. Dismissed."

Stifling his protest with a look of chagrined anger, Private Mansfield snapped to attention, giving a stiff salute which Private First Class Holland echoed. Returning the salutes, Lieutenant Daniels took a breath, and then walked into the mess tent. "Sergeant Piper, Lance Corporal Masters, Lieutenant Kentworthy, Sergeant First Class Lyman, and Sergeant Bellamy, please report to Captain Morgan's tent."

Exchanging startled glances, the men scrambled to their feet, following him to the command tent, where Captain Morgan was in the process of being briefed by Corporal Winters, Petty Officer Reese standing behind him. Turning as the men entered the tent, Captain Morgan nodded. "All right, Corporal. Lieutenant Daniels, I take it you are in on this as well?"

Standing to attention, Lieutenant Daniels saluted, his voice crisp. "Only insofar as I was instructed by Petty Officer Reese's superior to gather these men, Sir!"

Returning the salute, Captain Morgan eyed the group gathered in his tent. "Well, then, I trust the group you mentioned will be arriving soon?"

As if on cue, the tent flap swept back and the Private on duty entered, with the man from the perimeter following him. "Sir, this man want s to see you. He says it's urgent, Sir."

Waving the sentry off, Captain Morgan faced the stranger with an ironic smirk. "So, you must be the one sending my officers running around the camp like crickets on a hot griddle. Well, you've got my attention now, so spit out what you came here for."

His face calm, the stranger pointed at the group of soldiers to his left. "Well, not to put to fine a point on it, Captain, but I've come for them. Allow me to explain," he continued hastily as Captain Morgan's eyebrows lowered in irritation and the soldiers shifted in surprise. "I'm here because over the last eight to ten months we have been watching this unit off and on, and several of your men have stood out to us with better than average jungle warfare skills; namely the men in this tent right now. I finally managed to regain contact, and I'm here to offer them a chance at transferring to the Special Observation Group."

Captain Morgan raised one eyebrow as he glanced over the faces of the men assembled. "That's a pretty tall order; you'd be taking some of my best men here. I'm not entirely sure I want to part with them."

Nodding understandingly, the stranger snapped off a crisp salute. "Very well then, Captain. I understand completely. If you change your mind, I will be maintaining some degree of contact. Good night, gentlemen. Sergeant."

With Petty Officer Reese in tow, he ducked out of the tent, rapidly vanishing into the darkness beyond the perimeter. Looking around at the men, Captain Morgan shrugged. "What are you all standing around in here for? You think this is a party? Dismissed!"

With a flurry of salutes, they quickly exited the tent, standing around for a moment outside as they conferred in low tones. "Where did that guy come from?" asked Lance Corporal Masters. Lieutenant Daniels shrugged. "Ask Kit; he's the one who was talking with that 'Petty Officer' character on the perimeter when I got there."

As all eyes turned to Corporal Winters, he gave a shrug of his own. "I don't know a lot about him, except that his name is Petty Officer Reese; I don't know his given name, he never told me; and that he's a SEAL working with the Special Observation Group, under the command of that guy we got the recruitment speech from."

Lieutenant Daniels felt a chill sliding down his spine as he stared after the retreating figure, Corporal Winters's words playing back in his head. If there are SEALs around here, then Hell itself is loose in these jungles. Oblivious to his superior's thoughts, Corporal Winters continued. "They've been conducting operations near and over the border, and they were hoping we would transfer as they need some reinforcements. It would take some training in the finer points of what they do, but obviously if they're trying to recruit us hard enough that they sent one of their guys into our camp to talk to Captain Morgan, and they know all of our names, ranks, and unit affiliation, then clearly we've got something the rest of Dog Company; heck, the rest of the battalion, doesn't have."

As various affirmative responses circulated, Lieutenant Daniels broke in. "All right, that's great, we're all a bunch of hotshots, but Corporal Winters, you have a sentry rota to complete with twenty minutes on the end to make up for time lost, and the rest of you had better be either hitting sentry duty yourselves or else hitting the rack. Good night, gentlemen."

Heading back to his hole, he wrapped himself up in his blanket, and fell into a light sleep until Sergeant Bellamy's hand on his shoulder awakened him in the morning. From the look on his face, he had news, and it wasn't good. "Fourth Battalion's Bravo Company hit de hilltop yesterday, and dey got in a fight with de enemy. We are being sent in to relieve dem today."

Stifling a yawn, Lieutenant Daniels began rolling up his blanket. "Thanks for the news, Sergeant. Have the men prepare to move."

Nodding, Sergeant Bellamy began awakening the men and informing them of the move. As they packed their gear, they noticed the Company commanders of 1/503 heading for Lieutenant Colonel Schumacher's command tent for the mission briefing.

Indicating the map, Lieutenant Colonel Schumacher began outlining the plan. "All right, we're going to move to relieve Bravo Company, and then divide into two task forces; Task Force Black and Task Force Blue. Black will consist of Charlie Company and First and Third platoons of Dog, with Captain McElwain in command of the overall task force and Captain Morgan in command of the two platoons of Dog. Blue will consist of Alpha Company and Second Platoon of Dog Company. Task Force Black will move to find and destroy the PAVN forces who ambushed Bravo Company, with Task Force Blue securing the hill and then moving to support Task Force Black."

Captain Morgan raised his hand. "Sir, correct me if I'm wrong, but didn't Colonel Livsey recommend that we deploy in battalion strength at minimum, to help mitigate our losses?"

Lieutenant Colonel Schumacher's eyes hardened. "The Colonel and I don't see eye to eye on this issue, and since he's not here, he can't object to my plans."

Captain Morgan and Captain McElwain looked at each other, and Captain McElwain opened his mouth, but Lieutenant Colonel Schumacher cut him off. "The Colonel isn't used to dealing with elite troops. We're Airborne, not some ground-pounder herd. We could march across this entire Highland on our own, and kick the guts out of any PAVN unit unfortunate enough to cross our path. I need you gentlemen to remember that, and act like it, especially in front of the men. What you think, and how you act, is how they're going to think and act. If you think that we're going to get our teeth kicked in, then they're probably going to get their teeth kicked in. But if you act like we're going to kick the crud out of each and every last gook we come across, then that's probably what's going to happen."

Straightening from where he bent over the map, he nodded. "Good luck, gentlemen. Let's get this thing done."

Coming to attention and snapping off a crisp salute, Captain Morgan exited the tent, wondering if Lieutenant Colonel Schumacher was right, or if his customary battle recklessness was taking over again.

Jumping out of the helicopter, Lieutenant Daniels led the rest of the platoon as they dashed into a defensive perimeter, waiting out the landing phase and keeping their eyes and weapons up as the Hueys beat the air and rose into the air once again. Almost immediately upon their landing, Captain McElwain began pushing forward with Task Force Black, searching for the elusive foe that had engaged Bravo Company. Pushing forward, they encountered nothing on the first day, and set up camp. The next morning, the clearing patrol discovered communication wire, and the Task Force began moving forward as the point man from First Platoon, Charlie Company tramped through the brush, his eyes on the cable. "It took a turn here, Sir. It's still going in the same general direction; it's..." Suddenly his voice trailed off. From behind him, Lieutenant Keyes, the commander of First Platoon, called out. "It's what, Private?"

His rifle up and off safety, the point man raised his voice slightly. "It's attached to a gook, Sir, and he's still alive. I can see him staring right at me."

As Lieutenant Keyes came crashing through the brush to investigate, a bugle suddenly sounded in the trees and brush ahead of them, followed by a series of whistles as a pack of screaming PAVN soldiers broke cover and came charging at them. "Form a defensive perimeter!" shouted Lieutenant Daniels, his words echoed by nearly every officer in the unit as Task Force Black prepared to fight for its life. Mortars rained down from the enemy positions, machine guns laced the air with tracers, and rockets came hurtling in from all directions, sending up gouts of dirt and debris, but mostly missing their intended targets. Hugging the ground, Lieutenant Daniels forced his head up just below the whirring bullets to see a wall of PAVN soldiers charging at them. Rolling over onto his back, he squirmed around so that his feet were facing the enemy, and began firing his rifle at them on full-auto as the men around him began following suit. A pair of explosions crashed in the enemy line as two of the platoon grenadiers got into action, and the familiar rattling chatter of the M60 reverberated as the machine guns began to voice their opinion regarding the ambush. Hit with a withering barrage at close range, the charge stalled, then broke and retreated, beginning to fire from a safer distance. As Dog Company's two platoons began moving carefully to join the perimeter; having been outside the main area where Charlie Company was making the main defense position; Lieutenant Keyes called over to Private Lecter, the point man who had discovered the enemy position. "Hey, what happened to that gook you found on the cable?"

Private Lecter looked as if Keyes had lost his mind. "I shot him, Sir!"

Crawling behind his platoon line, Lieutenant Daniels called encouragement as he popped up to loose brief bursts of fire at the enemy before dropping back to the ground and continuing forward along the embattled perimeter.

It soon became painfully obvious that they were under attack from a sizable enemy force, and that they were not going to cut and run like they had been all along. Getting to the radio, Captain McElwain called the CO of Task Force Blue. "Blue Six, Blue Six, this is Black Six. We are under heavy enemy assault and pinned down. Requesting urgent reinforcement, over!"

"Roger that, Black Six. Task Force Blue is on its way.

Blue Six out."

Changing magazines, Lieutenant Daniels crawled over to Lance Corporal Masters. "How are you doing for ammo?"

Glancing at Private Mansfield, his ammo bearer, Lance Corporal Masters passed on the query, then turned back to Lieutenant Daniels. "About four belts, Sir!"

Nodding, Lieutenant Daniels crawled on, reaching Private First Class Holland. "How are you doing for grenades?"

Sliding a round into his M79, Holland replied, "Thirty grenades, Sir."

Taking aim at an enemy machine gun position, he pulled the trigger, a gout of flame and debris rising from the target. "Twenty-Nine, Sir."

With a snort, Lieutenant Daniels moved further down the line, suddenly spotting a group of PAVN who were making another bid to break the line; charging forward under covering fire from a pair of machine guns. Waving frantically to Holland, he began firing his rifle at the front-runners, cutting several of them down as the nearby riflemen joined in. Scrambling into position, Private First Class Holland triggered a round that just missed the machine gun, but attracted the attention of the crew, who slewed it around and directed a volley of shots in his direction, sending him diving for the deck. Lieutenant Daniels was about to try and target them, when the gunner suddenly went down with two bullets in his chest, and the loader flopped to the ground with a shot to the head. Looking over, Lieutenant Daniels spotted Corporal Winters, his face devoid of emotion as he picked off three more of the charging infantrymen with his M14 rifle. Deprived of their covering fire, the enemy nonetheless continued their mad, desperate charge, the last of them making it to within five feet of Lieutenant Daniels, and killing one of the riflemen near him. An hour had gone by with no sign of Task Force Blue, and four of the men in Lieutenant Daniels's platoon were wounded, one killed. Making his way to Captain Morgan, he asked, "What's the status on Task Force Blue, Sir?"

His expression grim, Captain Morgan shook his head. "Word is they're pinned down worse than we are. Schumacher's trying to get someone into position to relieve us, but it's hard. I think they're moving Charlie Company from 4th Battalion to come get us out of here, but they're not doing so hot either."

Lieutenant Daniels nodded. "Understood, Sir. Any further orders? Will we be attempting a breakout?"

Captain Morgan shook his head again. "Our orders so far are to sit tight and hold on; wait for the relief column."

With another nod, Lieutenant Daniels saluted. "Yes, Sir. We'll hold 'em off."

Returning to his platoon in time to see another enemy assault crumble under a withering artillery barrage, he passed on the message. All along the line, the men nodded grimly, checked their ammunition, and braced themselves for the next attack. As the sun climbed past its zenith, the desperate battle continued, with almost constant enemy fire lashing the beleaguered company. During one of the close assaults, a PAVN soldier lobbed a grenade that landed near a group of wounded soldiers. Without hesitating, one of the men retrieving belts of machine gun ammunition nearby hurled himself on the grenade, the blast lifting him into the air for a brief second before he sprawled dead on the ground, less than three feet from the wounded men whose lives his sacrifice had preserved. Finally, around 1300 Hours, they could hear the sound of fighting from the direction of friendly lines as C Company fought their way through. The fighting lasted almost another hour, but finally the enemy retreated and they were able to withdraw to camp. As they regrouped, Captain Morgan turned to

Captain McElwain, a wry smile on his face. "I think we found those guys that were scrapping with Bravo Company; what do you think?"

Shaking his head at Morgan's attempt at humor, Captain McElwain headed for the helicopters, his mind on the twenty dead, one hundred and fifty-four wounded, and two missing that the operation had cost. As he alighted from the chopper, one of his men intercepted him. "Sir, regarding one of the casualties, I would like to recommend him for a decoration. It's Private First Class Barnes, Sir."

Captain McElwain cocked his head. "For what reason, Sergeant?"

the Sergeant's voice was calm, despite what he had to say. "Conspicuous gallantry, Sir. Private First Class Barnes had taken over an abandoned machine gun and was using it to repel a PAVN attack, when he ran out of ammunition. As he was retrieving more ammo, he saw that the enemy had just thrown a grenade near a group of wounded soldiers. He jumped on the grenade to save their lives."

Captain McElwain nodded. "I'll talk to the Colonel about it."

Returning to Lieutenant Colonel Schumacher's command tent, he saluted. "Task Force returned, Sir!"

Lieutenant Colonel Schumacher nodded. "At ease, Captain. Casualties?"

"Twenty killed; eight from Task Force Black. One hundred fifty four wounded, fifty seven from Task Force Black. Two missing from Charlie Company."

Lieutenant Colonel Schumacher's jaw clenched at the news, then he forced himself to relax. "Enemy body count? It had better be high, Captain."

Captain McElwain shook his head. "Eighty dead, Sir."

Rising to his feet, Lieutenant Colonel Schumacher shook his head violently, his voice one step off of a yell. "Eighty! That is absolutely unacceptable! Get back out there and re-count, Captain!"

Stunned, Captain McElwain started to protest, but Lieutenant Colonel Schumacher cut him off with a wave of his hand. "That's an order, Captain! Dismissed!"

Seething, Captain McElwain snapped off a frigid salute, executed a ramrod-straight about-face, and stalked out of the tent.

By nightfall the news was all over the camp. After reporting the body count, Captain McElwain had been ordered by Lieutenant Colonel Schumacher to go re-count; returning from the count, he had given a more palatable tally of one hundred and seventy five. Later on that day, when Captain McElwain recommended Private First Class Barnes for a decoration regarding his actions that day, Lieutenant Colonel Schumacher refused to endorse his recommendation. According to the sentry who had overheard the conversation, Lieutenant Colonel Schumacher was quoted as saying he "didn't think that medals were for men who committed suicide."

In the wake of the clashes between Lieutenant Colonel Schumacher and Captain McElwain, first over the body count and later over the decoration, Task Forces Black and Blue ("At least that's what we were when Charlie got through with us" was the sentiment of several soldiers in the aftermath) were dissolved, reverting to their original company formations. The night after the battle, Lieutenant Daniels was patrolling the sentry line with Sergeant Bellamy when he saw Kit standing on a low rise, watching a series of flashes of light, mixed with rumbles almost as of thunder, from the direction of Dak To Airfield; almost a mile away. "What's going on?"

Indicating the light and sound with a wave of his hand, Corporal Winters responded, "Looks like Charlie is trying to take out the airfield."

As the barrage continued, Sergeant Bellamy snorted. "Day hasn't come yet when Charlie had de weapons to take out our airfields."

No sooner were the words out of his mouth, when a colossal explosion rocked the ground, a fireball rising from the airfield as a roaring shockwave slammed into the men, knocking them to the ground with ringing ears. Spitting out dirt and blood from a bitten tongue and a burst lip, Lieutenant Daniels felt something warm and wet trickling down his upper lip, and wiped it off, discovering with a vague feeling of surprise that it was blood from his nose. With a massive effort, he pushed to his feet, looking around at the other men, who were looking similarly afflicted. For several minutes nobody said anything as they fought the ringing in their ears, then Lieutenant Daniels turned to Sergeant Bellamy with a sarcastic look on his face. "So, they don't have anything that could take out one of our airfields?"

Bellamy looked slightly off-kilter still, but nodded unsteadily. "Well, maybe dat was one of our things he hit."

After considering that for a moment, Lieutenant Daniels nodded. "All right, I'll buy that for the moment, but whatever that was, it was huge!"

The rest of the night passed uneventfully, and in the morning they received orders to scour the area of the battle with Task Force Black, and then move southeast to occupy Hill 882. As they prepared to move out, Lieutenant Daniels noticed a group of about a dozen civilians with camera equipment and notebooks gathering with the men. Approaching Captain Morgan, he exchanged salutes, his expression puzzled. "Sir, what are civilians doing here? We're moving out in less than ten."

His own expression taut, Captain Morgan nodded. "Yes, Lieutenant, I'm well aware of that fact. I am also aware that for reasons best kept to themselves, the higher brass have decreed that we're taking them with us on the op. If you're interviewed, no comment; pass it on to the men."

Nodding, Lieutenant Daniels hurried back to where Sergeant Bellamy and Corporal Winters were waiting. "Okay, those guys over there are reporters, and they're coming with us. If they interview us, we're to reply with 'No Comment'. Pass it on to the men."

As they began to pass the word, Lieutenant Daniels spotted one of the reporters heading in their direction. Walking to intercept him, he subtly placed himself between the men and the reporter. "Can I help you?"

Glancing at his rank insignia and name-tag, the reporter nodded, his expression bright and engaging. "Lieutenant, uh, Daniels? Yes, I was hoping I could get an off-the-record word on how things are going out here?"

Shaking his head, Lieutenant Daniels reminded himself to keep his face and voice calm and professional; non-threatening, but unyielding. "Sorry; no comment."

His face becoming frustrated for a moment before resuming its former cast, the reporter persisted. "Surely you have something to say; any thoughts on the way the battle a few days ago was handled, or about the body count controversy?"

Resisting the urge to ask what he was talking about, Lieutenant Daniels firmly shook his head. "Sorry; no comment."

Frustration finally overpowering his professional demeanor, the reporter shook his head in exasperation. "Ohhh, what's the use of talking to you dumb grunts!"

Letting a small smile out at the man's retreating back, Lieutenant Daniels turned back to his men, slinging his rifle briefly as he grabbed a couple of hand grenades sitting on a table in the supply area and slid them into his pockets. Rejoining his men, he waited patiently as the other two companies assembled, whereupon they moved out at a fast walk. Over the next two days, the reporters made several more attempts to buttonhole the soldiers, but Dog Company wasn't talking, and they turned their attention elsewhere. Finally, as the sun began rising above the tree-line on the second day, they began climbing the slopes of Hill 882. Dog Company was in the lead, with First Platoon on point as they crested the hill. Scanning the hilltop, Corporal Winters's eyes widened as he spotted the network of bunkers ahead of him. Turning, he dropped into a half-crouch, shouting a warning to the rest of the platoon. "Contact Front; hostile fortifications! Get down, get down!"

Dropping to the ground as he shouted, the company began passing on the warning to the rest of the battalion amid a withering barrage of machine gun fire pouring from the bunkers. Returning fire, the rest of the battalion rushed to take cover and assume defensive positions. Setting up an aid station below the crest of the hilltop, Captain Morgan had the reporters shepherded to safety in the aid station and then began directing fire against the heavily fortified enemy positions. As he was calling in an artillery strike against the enemy positions, the medic ran up to Captain Morgan, the acting commander of the unit as Captain McElwain was out of favor with Lieutenant Colonel Schumacher and Captain Kemper's replacement was still experientially junior to Morgan. "Captain, we've got wounded here that are going to need immediate medevac; we need choppers now!"

Nodding, Captain Morgan grabbed the radio. "Sky One Six, Sky One Six, this is Dog Six. We need an immediate Dust Off, do you read me, over?"

Lieutenant Colonel Schumacher's voice was unyielding. "Dog Six, I read you, and there are helicopters inbound but you need to use them to get the reporters to safety first, is that clear?"

Shocked, Captain Morgan gaped at the radio for a moment before replying. "But Sir, these men will die without care, and the reporters-"

Lieutenant Colonel Schumacher interrupted him, his voice savage. "I said the reporters go out first, Captain; and that's an order! Get them out, and then we can worry about your men getting evacuated. Is that clear?!"

Captain Morgan nearly blew his top at that point, but arguing would avail him nothing, so he bit his tongue for a long moment before responding. "Understood Sir. And Sir? They're your men too. Dog Six out."

Slamming the handset back into the cradle, he turned back to the anxious medic. "No dice, Doc. Lieutenant Colonel Schumacher said we gotta get the reporters out first, and then worry about the wounded. I'm sorry, Doc, but when those helicopters come, we gotta get the reporters on board first."

The medic stared at him for a moment, then said something that quite plainly, if not very politely, stated his opinion of the decision before turning back to the aid station. Almost twenty minutes later, the clattering whump of helicopters brought most of the men's heads up, some in hope, others, who knew the truth about what they were here for, in bitter condemnation of the one giving the order. As they landed, Alpha Company's 2nd Platoon began moving the reporters toward the waiting choppers, an order that Lieutenant Knightley was loath to give but they were quick to obey. As the choppers were lifting off, the crew chief on the last chopper ran over to the senior medic. "We got room for three stretchers if you've got urgent casualties!"

His face lighting with swift relief, the medic nodded, turning to his team and yelling orders as they prepped the three most grievously wounded soldiers for transport.

Watching them lift off, he shook his head, then turned back to his duties.

Grabbing an M72 LAW rocket launcher, Sergeant Bellamy took aim at the nearest bunker, firing and then dropping the launcher as he dived for cover. The round impacted solidly on the front of the bunker, blowing it apart and exposing the surviving occupants to a hail of bullets from the trio of riflemen behind him, but in the next minute, two of them went down from a machine gun in the adjoining bunker. As Bellamy laid down covering fire, the other soldier grabbed one of the men, and another rifleman dashed over to lift the second, carrying them clear and heading for the aid station. As the next wave of helicopters came in, these ones loaded with water and ammunition, Captain Morgan gave a sigh of relief, mingled with stifled wrath at the reason some of the men were still here when they should have gone out with the first wave of choppers, and could have if not for Lieutenant Schumacher's order. All along the line, the men increased their fire on the enemy bunkers, trying desperately to suppress the PAVN soldiers and make safe the landing for the brave, or crazy, Huey pilots as they swooped in through a blistering barrage of bullets to drop off urgently needed water and ammunition, and evacuate the wounded. As the day wore on, the sun beat down mercilessly on the vicious battle raging on the crest of Hill 882. The 81mm mortars were under heavy fire from the enemy mortar positions, and began a savage duel with them in an attempt to silence them, while on the front lines, the 60mm mortars battered at the enemy bunkers and trenches in concert with sporadic M79 fire. The fighting followed much the same pattern until evening, when a sudden chorus of whistles blew from the enemy positions, followed by a group of screaming PAVN soldiers that popped up out of the forward trench positions to charge the American line.

Switching to airburst rounds, the mortars began cutting up the charge, as the machine guns and rifles finished the job at the cost of three more wounded. After that, the battle seemed to wind down for the night; with a few shots fired, but nothing more until dawn, when yet another charge had to be broken up by the groggy soldiers with mortar and machine gun fire. That seemed to be the signal for the day to begin for the enemy, as they began a vicious fire on the battalion, which was returned wholeheartedly by the Americans. As Lieutenant Daniels was checking on his men, Platoon Sergeant Bellamy, who had been running along behind him, suddenly fell to the ground with a cry of pain. Turning, Lieutenant Daniels saw a rosette of blood spreading along his upper arm. Running over, he began to help the wounded Sergeant to his feet, but Bellamy waved him off angrily. Pulling out his first aid kit, Lieutenant Daniels began tying a bandage around Sergeant Bellamy's arm. "Are you okay?"

Bellamy's face was red with wrath. "Je suis fâched!"

Raising his eyebrows, Lieutenant Daniels caught the gist of the meaning from Platoon Sergeant Bellamy's tone, and let him get to his feet unassisted. "Seriously, though, does it hurt?"

Sergeant Bellamy growled under his breath in Cajun for a moment before replying. "Nah, I've hurt worse from a taon."

At Lieutenant Daniels's questioning look, he explained as they continued moving along the line. "Biting fly from de bayous. Nasty little guys."

Tyler was running low on ammunition; down to two belts; and several other men were running low. Sending a soldier back to the supply area for ammo, Lieutenant Daniels continued down the line, pausing every so often to fire on the enemy positions where resistance seemed thickest. As he was nearing the aid station, he noticed that the blood spreading along the bandage hadn't stopped, but had almost covered the entire bandage. Stopping Sergeant Bellamy with a hand on his uninjured arm, he began pushing him towards the aid station. "That wound isn't looking so good, Sergeant. I think we need to have it looked at by a professional."

Sergeant Bellamy shook his head in protest, but his words were cut off with a gasp of pain as Lieutenant Daniels accidentally put his hand on the injury. Rolling his eyes, Lieutenant Daniels half-shoved, half-pulled him down the hill; arriving at the aid station, he was intercepted by a medic. "Where's he hit?"

Gesturing at the bloody bandage on Bellamy's bicep, Lieutenant Daniels shook his head. "Upper arm; he says it's not that bad, but if you could just check it out?"

Nodding, the medic quickly cut the bandage away to reveal an ugly gash running from just above his elbow to midway up his arm. His breath hissing between his teeth at the sight, the medic had Bellamy lie down while he cleaned, disinfected, stitched, and bandaged the injury. "All right, that should do it. Just don't do anything crazy."

Lieutenant Daniels exchanged a look with Sergeant Bellamy, then looked back at the medic. "Oh, don't worry, Doc, he won't. If he does, we'll be back."

Leaving the medic working out what they meant, and then trying to call them back, the two men ran for the battle line, stopping by the supply depot and loading up on ammunition on the way. The rest of the day was spent in much the same pattern; alternately helping direct fire on the enemy, and running supplies to the men. As evening fell on the third day with no sign of either side withdrawing, Lieutenant Daniels was walking the perimeter when he ran into Lieutenant Kentworthy and Sergeant Piper. Sergeant Piper appeared completely unruffled, calmly puffing on a cigar, but Lieutenant Kentworthy sported a bandage on his forehead and had a slightly harried look about him. Lieutenant Kentworthy indicated the bandage with a wave of his hand. "What happened to you?"

Lieutenant Kentworthy didn't respond for a second, his eyes flickering two and fro, then fixed on Lieutenant Daniels. "Huh? Oh. Um, I forgot to duck."

As he fell silent again, Sergeant Piper spoke up. "He means he got his fool head sliced up by a hand grenade that blew when he was sticking his head up to see if it really was a hand grenade. It was."

Nodding distractedly, Lieutenant Kentworthy suddenly snapped into focus again, turning to Sergeant Piper. "Ed, put that out. You should know better than to smoke after dark; it makes you a target for any sniper within three hundred meters."

Sighing regretfully, Sergeant Piper stubbed out his cigar, sticking it back in his mouth. "Sorry Sir, it just kind of crept up on me; sundown, I mean."

With another nod, Lieutenant Kentworthy shook himself, seeming to come back to the present. "It's okay; just don't forget near me. How are your men holding up, Carl?"

Lieutenant Daniels shrugged, waving his hand at Sergeant Bellamy, who was cleaning his rifle while Tyler watched the enemy line from behind his freshly-cleaned M60; as night fell, the men took the opportunity to clean their weapons and eat in shifts; one man cleaning his weapon or eating while another stood guard. "As well as can be expected, given the state of affairs right now. Any word from higher-up whether we're going to be pulling out any time soon?"

Lieutenant Kentworthy shook his head. "I just talked to Captain Morgan this afternoon, and he said Lieutenant Colonel Schumacher wants to push Charlie off this hill come what may."

Nodding, Lieutenant Daniels exchanged salutes, beginning to turn back towards his own men. As Sergeant Piper turned to follow Lieutenant Kentworthy back along the line, however, he found his arm grabbed, and he was spun around to face Lieutenant Daniels. "Sergeant, is the Lieutenant squared away? When I was talking to him, he seemed pretty shook up about something. What's going on?"

Sergeant Piper took his cigar from his mouth and stared at the dead end for a moment before replying. "Well, for one thing, there was that grenade, for another, there's the fact that we had to pull those blasted civilians out before our own wounded and one of 'em was the Lieutenant's best M60 gunner, and for a third, he hasn't slept in almost sixty-two hours. I'm going to see if I can convince him to catch some rack time and let me do the perimeter patrols by myself tonight."

Turning away, he stuck the cigar back in his mouth and marched off after Lieutenant Kentworthy. Shaking his head, Lieutenant Daniels turned his own steps back along his line, to where Sergeant Bellamy was waiting. "What was dat about?"

Lieutenant Daniels shrugged. "Just checking in on the state of affairs with our brother platoon, and seeing if they knew about our projected activities on this Command-forsaken lump of Terra Firma. Apparently we're supposed to hold on at all costs, and drive the enemy from the hill."

Sergeant Bellamy nodded, as if that was the answer he had been expecting. "And de platoon?"

Lieutenant Daniels hesitated for a moment before replying, weighing his words carefully; what he should and should not say. "Well, Sergeant Piper forgot to put out his cigar, which ticks the Lieutenant off because of possible enemy snipers."

Sergeant Bellamy grinned. "Yeah, dat would tick me

off too. Anything else?"

Lieutenant Daniels shook his head. "Nothing that needs talking about. I'm going to hit the rack; wake me up in two hours."

His perceptions fogged by the stress and exertion of the day, it seemed to Lieutenant Daniels that he had just closed his eyes when Sergeant Bellamy was shaking him awake. "Two hours, Sir."

Grinding the heels of his hands into his eyes to dispel the feeling of having his eyelids coated with sandpaper, Lieutenant Daniels sat up, grabbing his boots and shaking them upside down to ensure there was nothing inside. Expelling a wandering centipede from his left boot, he laced them on, picking up his rifle as he rose to his feet. "All right, Sergeant, hit the rack. I'll wake you up in two hours."

Nodding, Sergeant Bellamy headed for his bedroll as Lieutenant Kentworthy made the rounds of the sentries. At dawn, they woke the men, bracing for the morning attack that had shaken them awake the day before, but instead of the expected charge, the PAVN forces opted to open the ball with a shower of mortar rounds and rockets that sent them diving for what little cover their was to be had. As another air strike bathed the morning gloom in a wash of orange-red light from the napalm coating the enemy bunkers, another flight of Hueys came clattering in with ammunition and other supplies. Offloading as quickly as possible through the vicious crossfire created by the PAVN forces and Americans, they took off again with two of their number streaming smoke from enemy fire. As the Hueys departed over the tree line, Sergeant Lyman suddenly gave a grunt and went down, clutching at his chest. Racing over, his heart sinking, Lieutenant Kentworthy fumbled with the last of his bandages, hollering for a medic. As he searched for an injury, Sergeant Lyman suddenly sat up. "Aaaagh!"

Startled by the cry of pain, Lieutenant Daniels rocked back on his heels. "Where are you hit?"

One hand going to his jacket pocket, a look of emotional torment crossed Sergeant Lyman's face. "Right in the chess board, Sir!"

Lieutenant Daniels looked nonplussed as the medic came charging towards them. "The chess board?"

Nodding painfully, Sergeant Lyman reached into the chest pocket of his jacket, pulling out the fractured ruins of a folding chess board. "The chess board, Sir! The one your wife gave me for Christmas last year! I was carrying it in my pocket, and the bullet hit it."

Sliding to his knees, the medic began pulling his satchel around to the front of his body. "Where are you hit, Sergeant?"

Lyman shook his head, his expression pained. "This chess board stopped the bullet, Doc; but I think it cracked a rib or two."

Checking the injury, the medic nodded. "Yep. You've probably got two cracked ribs, maybe three, but you'll live."

The battle raged on with unrelenting ferocity until approximately noon, when the tempo of the PAVN fire seemed to be slackening off. By mid-afternoon, it became clear that the enemy was in the final stages of withdrawing, and Captain Morgan radioed Lieutenant Colonel Schumacher with the news that Hill 882 was secure. Returning to the airbase at Ben Het, they noticed the absence of the Second and Fourth Battalions; upon inquiry they were informed that they were in the process of taking Hill 875. For three days, they received no further official word about what was happening in the battle for the hill; although the fighters roaring by overhead, and the helicopters that either returned with severe battle damage or didn't return at all told their own grim tale; but then on the 24th, they began seeing the helicopters returning loaded with wounded. Intercepting one of the platoon leaders, Lieutenant Daniels asked, "What happened out there?"

His expression haunted, the young Lieutenant shook his head. "They wiped us out, man. They were waiting for us; just wiped us out."

Unable to get anything further out of him, Lieutenant Daniels abandoned the interrogation, but not the search for information, which was not long in forthcoming. It turned out that in the course of the battle, they had lost one-fifth of the 173rd's total combat strength in killed, wounded, or missing. With many of its units combat ineffective, the 173rd was being transferred to Camp Radcliff to rest and refit.

As they were packing up, the man who had spoken to them about joining the Special Observations Group appeared at the door of the barracks. "Heard about what happened with the 2nd and 4th Battalions. My condolences."

Lieutenant Daniels shrugged. "Yeah; that was pretty rough. I imagine you didn't come here just to offer your condolences, though. What do you want?"

With a millimetric smile, the man nodded, stepping inside as though Lieutenant Daniels's question had been an invitation to come in. "As a matter of fact, I wanted to let you know that the offer is still on the table. Since you're going to be rotated out of active combat duty, I presumed that you would not be missed if you were to transfer. It would require some training, but I feel reasonably confident that you would be ready for operations by early next year. What do you say?"

Lieutenant Daniels looked at the rest of the group; the men who had been offered the transfer with him; then back at the man. "Well, as long as Captain Morgan gives his okay, I don't see why not; at least, not now, anyway."

The man nodded briskly. "Splendid! I've already talked it over with Captain Morgan, and he said that since you were heading for rest and refitting, he saw no reason why he couldn't spare you all. I see you have your gear already packed; we leave in five minutes."

Looking at each other, the men quickly grabbed their bags and followed their new commander out the door to a waiting helicopter. On the way to the chopper, Sergeant Lyman dashed to the recreation hall, returning a moment later with the large wooden chess board that had graced one of the tables. Looking at him askance, Lieutenant Kentworthy asked, "Isn't that stealing?"

Sergeant Lyman shook his head. "Nope. This one's mine; I brought it from Bien Hoa; but I bring, well, brought, the travel chess set out on patrols."

A half an hour by helicopter brought them to a remote firebase near the Cambodian border that their commander; who went by the sobriquet 'Chief', used as a base of operations for his Hatchet Team. Petty Officer Reese and a squad of SEALs also based out of the camp, but they were much more rarely seen; by and large, SEALs operated on the coast and in the Mekong Delta. Upon arrival at the camp, they were assigned to a Hornet Team; the platoon-sized sub-unit of the Hatchet Team; under the command of a short, squat man in his mid-forties who went by Mad Dog and wore a perpetually ticked off expression. Looking them up and down, he scowled silently for a full minute before speaking, his voice sounding like tank treads over gravel. "All right, hotshots, I've gotta get you trained for my world so you don't get yourselves killed and me in the bargain."

The next five weeks were a blur of training in advanced jungle warfare, use of VC and PAVN weapon and tactics, prisoner Snatch And Grab or Grab And Terminate, setting and detection of booby traps, how to dismantle and reuse enemy booby traps, and limited counter-interrogation and escape techniques provided by Sergeant Reese and the SEALs. As they were training, the other members of the Team were bringing in and transmitting reports of indicators that the North Vietnamese were getting ready to launch some kind of major offensive in the near future. This information was corroborated by Spike Teams; the brave (some said crazy) teams of men who, in cooperation with ARVN special forces, conducted daring reconnaissance missions into Laos and Cambodia; but nobody higher-up appeared to be taking them particularly seriously. With the Tet Truce coming up, a lot of the ARVN officers and enlisted were already making plans for their Tet celebrations rather than paying attention to possible enemy offensives. A week before their training was complete, one of the other Hornet Teams returned with news that Saigon, Khe Sanh, and multiple other US bases had been pretty much simultaneously attacked. With a derisive snort, the intelligence and communications liaison from the CIA pushed his glasses higher on his nose. "They sent me here to assemble pertinent and cohesive intelligent reports-"

"Intelligence reports," corrected Pinball, the short, perpetually energetic leader of one of the other Hornet Teams. The analyst nodded absently. "Yeah, those too. Anyway, I'm supposed to assemble them from the intelligence-gathering expeditions of the field teams, and when I send on the reports, do they listen to me? Nooo, they say they know so much better, sitting in their air-conditioned offices in Saigon and Virginia, that I don't have the big picture. If that's the case, then why the heck do they have me stuck up here in the jungle typing up reports for them?!"

Pinball shrugged, bouncing on his toes for a moment, then beginning to pace. "I dunno. That's the CIA for you.

We gave them what they needed to know, and they didn't believe it, and now they're caught with their hand in a light-bulb socket for it."

Two weeks later, they were finally cleared for action, and got their first assignment; a raid on the Ho Chi Minh Trail to interdict enemy supplies and hopefully capture at least one prisoner for interrogation. Grabbing his CAR-15, Lieutenant Daniels was sliding grenades and magazines into his web gear when he noticed one of the other men placing a grenade high on his web vest, away from the rest. Looking quizzically at the grenade, Daniels indicated it with a wave of his hand. "What's that doing up there? You've still got room down with the rest of 'em."

Nodding grimly, the man grabbed two more grenades, sliding them onto the lower portion of his web vest. "Yep. But this one's special. It's the one I'll be using if it looks like I'm going to be captured."

Lieutenant Daniels's mouth opened, then shut, then re-opened. "You mean, you're going to blow yourself up if you get captured?"

The man nodded again. "Uh-huh. After seeing some of the stuff our buddies went through when they got captured, we all decided that we would rather take as many of them with us as we can rather than get captured."

As he turned and walked out of the building, Lieutenant Daniels looked after him for a long moment before picking up one of the grenades left on the table and sliding it into a slot on the shoulder of his web vest. Grabbing a Claymore Mine, he headed out of the building and joined the men at the gate, boarding the helicopters two hours before dusk, and arriving at the LZ half an hour later. As they approached the LZ and disembarked, however, intense automatic fire slashed across the open ground, sending them diving to the ground and returning fire. Five minutes into the battle, it became clear that the LZ was untenable, and they quickly withdrew back to the helicopters; in effect being 'shot off' of the LZ, and making their way to the secondary LZ. Disembarking without undue incident, they trekked into the jungle, reaching the edge of the Trail, across the Cambodian border, in the hour after dusk. Lying up for most of the day, they broke camp in the dawn hour, setting up an ambush with a trio of Claymore Mines aimed to form a deadly bowl of death within their dispersion pattern. Nothing happened that night, but the following night they hit pay dirt, with a convoy consisting of two trucks and about twelve bicycles loaded with supplies making its way down the trail. The truck triggered the middle Claymore, which was dead center on the trail and attached to a tripwire; and the other two Claymores took the porters behind the truck, shredding them in a blast of fire and fury. The few survivors broke and ran, but unfortunately for one of them, his path took him directly across Lance Corporal Masters's legs, and the irate Masters promptly flipped over, scissoring his legs and sweeping the fleeing target's feet out from under him. From his position to Masters's left, Corporal Winters pounced on him, but the lithe Vietnamese, fighting like a wild cat, pulled a bayonet and tried to stab Masters. From his position on top of the Vietnamese, Corporal Winters reacted instinctively, latching onto the knife arm and breaking the wrist as he got the knife away, but that didn't stop the enraged PAVN soldier. Driving an elbow into Corporal Winters's head, he yanked the knife back and drove it downward, aiming for Lance Corporal Masters's throat. Barely avoiding the lethal blade, Masters pulled his own knife, stabbing him in the chest several times. Pushing the dead man off of Masters, Corporal Winters looked from the body to Lance Corporal Masters, then shrugged. "Guess we're not getting that guy as a POW."

For several minutes they waited tensely as scattered

shots rang out in the Cambodian jungle, but finally the rest of the platoon returned, assisting one of their number who was wounded. As they regathered, Mad Dog turned his scowl on his second in command, a pale, blond young man code-named Blackbeard. "Well, it looks like we did an okay job this time. Get the men ready to go. We're moving out in three."

Hoisting the wounded man onto his shoulders, Lance Corporal Masters looked quizzically at Blackbeard. "Is he always this cranky, or is it just the fact that we're along for the ride that's ticking him off?"

Shaking his head sardonically, Blackbeard turned to the group of soldiers rifling the truck for supplies or intel, waving them back from the trail and toward the regrouping unit. "Nah, he just talks like that all the time. You could have done the best job in the world, and he could be as happy as a lark, but he'd still look and sound just as cranky as he is right now. It's just who he is."

With the wounded soldier treated as best as they could under the circumstances and the rest of the unit regrouped, they began the trek back to the LZ, where the helicopters would take them back to base. As the weeks passed, it soon became clear that a massive offensive was underway all across South Vietnam, in an attempt to spark a popular rising. Something that was becoming equally obvious from the reports by the Spike Teams was that it was not going as expected; by and large, the South Vietnamese were not joining the revolution, but fighting against it, an outcome the North Vietnamese High Command had not anticipated. Something that was also becoming obvious was that their activities along the Ho Chi Minh Trail were making themselves felt. While on a raid into Cambodia, they were jumped by two divisions of PAVN soldiers, sparking a six-hour firefight before air strikes enabled them to disengage. However, the thick jungle and heavy ground fire prevented an extraction, turning the attempted retreat into a four-day running battle before they managed to go to ground and evade pursuit, leaving an uncounted number of dead PAVN soldiers in their wake. Undaunted by the counter-ambush, they headed out again the next week, aiming for a new section of the Trail to harass. Creeping up to the side of one of the many trails and jungle paths that made up the Ho Chi Minh Trail, Lieutenant Daniels reached into his pack, pulling out the components of a spike trap he had built. As he began reassembling it, the rest of the team were busy putting a punji deadfall back together with some nearby logs as weights; the only components they actually kept when they disassembled the enemy traps were the spikes, and occasionally some of the more complicated bits, like triggers; but for the most part they would simply trigger or disarm the traps and then make their own later. Although he was far less experienced than soldiers like Pinball, Blackbeard, Mad Dog, or Whiplash; a deceptively gangly-looking young man with the reflexes of a pit-viper who was the point man on many of the missions as well as the hands-down best at sentry removal; but he had taken to this kind of warfare like a duck to water, and was improving fast. Even Mad Dog had noticed, and given as much of a compliment as he ever gave: "Huh. Guess you didn't mess that up as bad as you could have."

The worst part of it for him was that he couldn't tell Rhiannon about what he was really doing; in his letters home, what he inferred, or on occasion had to outright tell her, was that he had survived unscathed when the unit was in some heavy fighting, and that they were rotated out of the combat zone for the moment, and leave it at that; so as far as she was concerned, the most danger he was in was when he went out on patrol and actually encountered the enemy; an occurrence he made out to be quite rare. Pulling his thoughts back to the present, he finished reassembling the trap, carefully arranging the foliage around the 'business end' and then backing away. Examining the spot, Blackbeard nodded. "Good."

Moving away from the trail, they moved further down, suddenly stopping a few yards into the jungle as they heard movement and low voices on the trail to their right. Automatically freezing, they looked at each other for a moment, then began easing their weapons loose. His eyes caught by a movement a few yards away, Corporal Winters held up a hand, clenching it into a fist. As the others stopped moving, he pointed in the direction from whence the movement had come, then signaled for movement, using the hand signals they had learned during their training. As the rest of the men signaled acknowledgement, he began walking toward the movement, only to drop to the ground as automatic weapons fire ripped through the trees and bushes, mingled with shouts and screams of pain. Waiting until the shooting stopped, the Hornet Team dashed forward, coming out onto an eerily familiar scene of massacre; the bodies of a platoon-sized, or possibly larger, unit of Vietnamese troops sprawled along the trail, along with some wrecked bikes loaded with supplies that were being busily picked over by a group of men in 'tiger stripe' jungle fatigues and camouflage face paint, who looked up with rifles at the ready when the men came into view. Relaxing a trifle as they recognized the Caucasian faces above the neutral uniforms; lacking any form of insignia, rank, or identifiers, so as not to give anything away if they were seen or captured/killed; the ambush party resumed rifling through the bags of supplies. Looking at each other, the members of the Hornet Team moved forward, Mad Dog calmly pulling the pin on an enemy grenade and wedging it under the body. With a shrug, the rest of the platoon began following suit, moving among the ambush party; which was comprised of three Americans and a half-dozen or so Vietnamese. One of them looked over at Lieutenant Daniels, who was showing some trepidation at booby-trapping the bodies. "You new at this?"

Shrugging, Lieutenant Daniels pulled a magazine loose, replacing it with an 'Italian Green' magazine loaded with explosive ammunition that had been created as a means of sowing suspicion and dissent between the North Vietnamese and their Russian suppliers. "Kinda. What's your name?"

The Green Beret stuck out his hand. "Staff Sergeant Bride. You?"

As Lieutenant Daniels was about to give his name and rank, Whiplash spoke up, cutting across his words. "That's Barracuda."

Indicating Lance Corporal Masters, Sergeant Bellamy, Corporal Winters, and Lieutenant Kentworthy, he continued. "That's Direwolf and Firedrake, over there is Raven, and we call him Kodiak."

Smirking, the American shook hands. "That kinda new; got it."

Firmly sealing his lips until they were on their way back to base, Lieutenant Daniels finally faced Whiplash. "So; I've got a code name, and so does the rest of the group, it would seem. Just when were you planning to tell us?"

Whiplash shrugged with his customary imperturbability. "About the time you needed to know; which was then. Just remember going forward, you're Barracuda, you're Direwolf, you're Raven, you're Kodiak, and you're Firedrake."

Mouthing his codename, Lieutenant Kentworthy was silent for a moment, and then spoke up. "So, how are these names assigned? Did I tick someone off, or is it that I just don't get a cool code name because you ran out before you hit my name on the list?"

Mad Dog half-turned, his usual look of displeasure

deeper than usual. "The code names are randomly generated and assigned. Don't feel so bad about yours; the Kodiak Bear is one of the biggest and fiercest of the Ursus family; I think the only one bigger may be a polar bear; maybe."

Weighing that over in his mind, Lieutenant Kentworthy shrugged acceptance and turned to Sergeant Lyman. "So what's his code name? Or doesn't he have one yet?"

Blackbeard kept his face to the front as he replied. "Gambit. And before you ask, yes, it really is randomly assigned, and no, most of the groups up here don't get code names. We're working more closely with the CIA than most, so we have code names generated by our liaison to help maintain a higher level of classification."

The next day they headed out again, managing to fight off the PAVN forces that they found at the Landing Zone, and moved toward the border. Pausing to listen, they suddenly heard something moving in the trees to their right, and instinctively formed a loose perimeter, eyes and ears straining to listen for anything remotely threatening in the seven-foot-tall elephant grass. A brief rustling sound was the only warning they had before automatic weapons fire began chopping through the grass all around them as hundreds of PAVN soldiers launched a furious ambush from three sides. The first few seconds were sheer, unmitigated madness as both sides hosed each other in a desperate fight for control, then everything fell silent, save for the click of metal and the rustle of cloth, as both sides ran out of ammunition and began to reload. Beating the Vietnamese to the punch, the Hornet Team managed to achieve fire superiority, but they were still hopelessly outnumbered. Unfortunately for the Vietnamese, they had left one side open, and that side led to a small hill; only about forty feet tall, but it was high ground. Moving at a dead run as they hosed the enemy, Lieutenant Daniels and his team made their way to the hill, firing in all directions as the enemy charged up the slopes toward them. Beating off one attack, then another, they switched to single-shot to conserve ammunition, hurling grenades to break up the worst of the attacks. Lying belly-down in the elephant grass, the green tracers of AK-47s zipping by overhead, Lieutenant Daniels looked over at Mad Dog, who was calmly calling in an air strike from the 'Covey', or special forces operator in the air control bird overhead. Twenty minutes of continuous exchange of fir followed, then the clattering of helicopter rotors sounded overhead as a pair of UH-1B gunships appeared on the horizon, swooping down on the enemy amid a blazing storm of fire from Miniguns, rocket pods, and M60 door guns; so close to the beleaguered team that they could see the brass falling from the machine guns. As enemy ground fire blazed back, the choppers rose and banked, heading for safety as tracers chased them across the sky. Before the enemy had time to raise a cheer, however, an A-1 Skyraider roared out of the blue to pummel them with machine gun fire and napalm. Raising a hand to shield his face, Mad Dog turned to Blackbeard and Whiplash. "That napalm's gonna light this whole field on fire! We gotta move!"

Leaving the enemy to burn in their wake, the Hornet Team raced off the hill towards the trees and away from the advancing flames; heat pushing at their backs and spurring them to greater urgency as they ran. Continuing their mad dash into the tree line, they finally stopped almost a half mile into the jungle, letting their breathing slow as they checked for signs of pursuit. Looking back at the blazing inferno that was the field of elephant grass, Blackbeard swallowed. "I don't think anything could have survived that."

Shaking his head, Whiplash swapped magazines on his CAR-15. "Nope. Crispy Critters all."

Moving out, they finally made it to the Trail, setting up an ambush consisting of a few 'toe-popper' mines in the trail and lines of short punji sticks covered with brush along the edges. Deploying along the sides of the trail, they concealed themselves, readied their weapons, and waited. For nearly six hours, nothing happened, and they were about ready to go find a more habited trail, when a company of PAVN came marching down the trail. Looking from the oncoming soldiers to the ambush point, Lieutenant Daniels considered trying to convince Mad Dog to call off the ambush, but there was no time. Just as he was starting to move backwards and crawl over to Mad Dog, the first 'toe-popper' went off under a soldier's foot, and the ambush 'mad minute' was on. Fury's own Madness broke loose in the quiet jungle as a wicked crossfire swarmed the enemy under, cutting them down in heaps where they stood, or tried to run. Grenades from the M79 Sergeant Piper now carried mixed with the deeper staccato beat of the M60 Lance Corporal Masters stubbornly refused to abandon despite the urgings and arguments of the rest of the team. For a few seconds, the hammering bedlam quieted slightly; broken by the uninterrupted fire of the M60; as the ambushers stopped to reload, then it picked right back up again where it had left off, beating out a requiem for the PAVN soldiers. As silence once again descended on the area, Mad Dog rose from his position, glancing around carefully before signaling for them to move on.

The next few weeks held similar levels of activity, with a few hair-raising moments as they were shot off of multiple Landing Zones, but unbeknownst to them, they had finally been tracked back to their base, and the North Vietnamese Command had decided to do something about them.

The first inkling they had that something was wrong

was when one of the perimeter Claymores went off; emplaced in the wire around the firebase, they were set to tripwire detonation, but theoretically far enough back that local fauna would not set them off. That could only mean that someone was attempting to cross or cut the wire; a very bad thing for the occupants of the camp. In the next second, the sentry began firing the M2 .50 Caliber machine gun, yelling about gooks on the wire. Running out of the barracks where he had been playing chess with (and being thoroughly beaten by) Sergeant First Class Lyman, Lieutenant Daniels dived into a foxhole, joined a second later by Corporal Winters. Amid a hail of rockets, a veritable horde of PAVN soldiers came charging across the open ground, a lucky, or well-aimed, shot taking out the M2 as the gunner was reloading. Despite fierce resistance, it soon became obvious that a breach of the perimeter was imminent, and several of them began falling back to secondary defense positions, the mess hall one of them. As the PAVN came swarming into the camp, rifle fire opened up on them at point-blank range from a half-dozen reinforced positions inside the wire. Firing from his position by one of the mess hall windows, Sergeant First Class Lyman paused to reload. Suddenly the door crashed open under the blast of a rocket, killing two of the SEALs near the door, and wounding one of the others. Through the smoke and debris, three enemy soldiers came bounding into the room, bayoneting the wounded soldier before he had time to bring his weapon into action. As the last SEAL in the room shot two of the invaders, the third shot him, then turned his weapon on Lyman. Hurling his weapon aside as it gave a hollow click, the PAVN soldier advanced on Lyman with a flying spin kick that just barely missed his face, and then launched a jumping double kick that knocked his rifle out of his hand and knocked him backwards. Falling back onto the table where he had been playing chess, Sergeant First Class Lyman grabbed a handful of the pieces and threw them into his opponent's face, distracting him long enough for Lyman to roll across the table and put a barrier between them. Looking around desperately for a weapon as the smaller man leaped onto the table, launching another kick that he barely dodged, Sergeant First Class Lyman snatched up the chess board and hit his opponent with the edge of the board in the ankle, knocking him off of the table and onto the floor. As he rolled to his back, groaning, Sergeant First Class Lyman dashed around the table, arriving just in time for his opponent to get to his knees and launch a punch. Catching the punch on the flat of the board, which broke under the impact, Lyman wielded the two broken halves, knocking aside the next punch with one and clobbering the PAVN soldier in the side of the head with the other. As the soldier staggered under the impact, almost falling, Sergeant First Class Lyman whacked him in the ribs with one half and stabbed the broken corner of the other half into his opponent's neck, leaving it in the wound and using the other half to drive it further in. As the man dropped to the ground, Sergeant First Class Lyman bent double and threw up, wiping blood spray and bile from his face. Behind him, the rest of the garrison began running toward the Mess Hall as they finished off the last of the attackers and noticed the breached door; stopping in the doorway as they viewed the charnel house that was the interior, they stood for some minutes in silence. Finally Lieutenant Daniels spoke up. "First that travel set, and now your big one. Jeez, what do these guys have against chess?"

Weak though it was, the joke seemed to lift the mood, drawing laughs from the rest of the men, Sergeant First Class Lyman included.

As the offensive progressed, it was becoming clear that there was a major command nexus operating in the Central Highlands, probably in the Giai Lai or one of the immediately surrounding provinces. As the Spike Teams were narrowing down the area where the nexus was located, word came down from high command: With resources stretched as thin as they were, Hatchet Team Three Thirty-Six would be sent after the command nexus. Finally, in October, they got a hit from a prisoner they extracted from the Giai Truong Son Highlands: the nexus was located in the same province as that from which she had been extracted. Gathering the Team in the briefing room, Chief began outlining the plan. "All right; we will be using two Hornet Teams; one for insertion, one for exfiltration security. Mad Dog's Hornet Team will conduct the insertion and prisoner securing, and Pinball's team will cover the exfiltration. This one's important enough that we will be having a helicopter extraction team. Our target is a Colonel in the PAVN believed to be conducting and coordinating operations in the Central Highlands; his name is currently unknown, so he will be code-named Butcher One. Our goal is to extract him and any of his close staff we can get along with any intelligence and documents we can find. For the infiltration, we will be dropped in twenty kilometers from the camp, and then move in. It has two gates, and barbed wire fencing around the perimeter. One guard tower with a pair of guards; two more guards at each gate. The helicopters will be on standby; no more than an hour from any LZ; but you have to get to an LZ they can use. Favorable Landing Zones are on the map here, here, here, and here; X-Ray, Charlie, Lima, and Sierra. Memorize these points, and the routes to them. Any questions?"

No one responded, and he nodded. "Good. Now make no mistake; retrieving Butcher One alive is the top priority, but if you can get any other personnel or documents, do it. Good luck gentlemen."

Heading out for a final equipment check, the two teams

quickly boarded the helicopters, traveling to the insertion point in silence. The sun was setting as they disembarked, pelting into the jungle and listening to the sound of the choppers growing fainter in the distance as they trekked toward the camp. Arriving just after midnight, they waited as Pinball's team deployed, ready to cover their retreat, and then moved in. A suppressed submachine gun took care of the guards in the tower and by the gate, and then the raiding party swarmed the gate, with two of the men; Roulette and Sherlock; taking up position to imitate the dead gate guards. Slipping into the officers barracks, the raiding party quickly began looking for the man matching the rough description passed on to them by various prisoners; working from shielded flashlights aimed at the floor or ceiling to provide increased ambient light, it took time. Suddenly, as they were checking the fourth person, one of the other men stirred, throwing the blankets back as he sat up. Dropping to the ground, the team quickly squirmed under beds or behind boxes as the man headed for the latrine; as he was coming back, Whiplash suddenly materialized behind him, clamping a hand over his mouth and placing a razor-sharp combat knife against his throat. As he froze, Lieutenant Kentworthy shined the small flashlight in the prisoner's face, giving a low grunt of recognition. "It's him."

Rising from beside the beds they had been hiding under, Sergeant Bellamy, Lieutenant Daniels, and Sergeant Bellamy quickly grabbed two more prisoners, converging back on the shadows next to the parade ground as Mad Dog and Blackbeard emerged from the command hut where they had been searching for documents; from the look on Blackbeard's face, it had been a success; Mad Dog looked as though the whole operation was going to ruin in a hand basket, as usual. As they made their way back through the gate, Lieutenant Daniels allowed himself a small sigh of relief: a picture-perfect operation; in and out and nobody's the wiser. His relief was premature. Even as he was thinking the triumphant thoughts, a sentry on the other gate called a challenge at them, followed by a droning wail as he began cranking an air-raid siren to rouse the camp. "That's torn it; let's move! Direwolf, take Butcher One; Barracuda, you, Whiplash, and Raven are rear-guard; Kodiak, you and Sorcerer take the prisoners!" muttered Mad Dog as he turned and loosed off a burst of shots at the sentry. Throwing Butcher One over his shoulder, Lance Corporal Masters turned and began to run as Lieutenant Kentworthy and Sergeant Piper; code name Sorcerer; followed suit. As they began to move towards the extraction points, it quickly became clear that Lima, Sierra, and Charlie were all blocked off by PAVN forces hunting them; and that only a monumental effort by Pinball's team was keeping X-Ray open. Getting on the radio on the morning of the second day, Blackbeard called the extract helicopters. "Cowboy Leader, Cowboy Leader, this is Blackbeard. Lima is blown; I say again, Lima is blown; X-Ray's gotta be it, requesting pickup, over."

"Roger that, Blackbeard, Cowboy Flight is inbound; ETA thirty mikes, out."

Signing off, Blackbeard nodded to Mad Dog. "They're coming; thirty minutes."

As they began heading for Landing Zone X-Ray, sudden enemy fire rattled among them, hitting one of the prisoners in the leg. Dropping to the ground and returning fire, the team was quickly pinned down and in danger of being surrounded. Getting back on the radio, Blackbeard began calling in an artillery strike. "Thunder-God, Thunder-God, this is Blackbeard. Fire Mission, X-Ray Tango, Two-Four-One, Zero-Three-Two, One-Nine-Five degrees, over."

As the fire control officer acknowledged, the smoke round came in squarely on target. "Fire for effect, over."

Almost forty-five seconds passed, and then a dozen or so shells came howling in, silencing the enemy on their flank. As a second fire mission wiped out the other party of enemy soldiers, they made their way to the Landing Zone, which was crawling with PAVN soldiers. Amid the crack and whine of bullets zipping by overhead, mingled with the sudden explosions of hand grenades, Blackbeard called the helicopter pilots. "Cowboy Leader, Cowboy Leader, this is Blackbeard! Be advised, this will be a hot extract, over!"

"Roger that, Blackbeard, ETA five mikes; out."

The minutes crawled by as they waited for the helicopters, but finally the spirit-lifting whomp-whomp-whomp of the chopper blades sounded over the roar of battle as the helicopters came over the tree line like massive birds of prey; hovering briefly as rockets and Minigun fire reached hungrily for the enemy soldiers in the trees. As the transport helicopters landed; the gunships still circling and dealing death to the enemy around them, Mad Dog waved them forward. "Let's go, let's go!"

Eyes on the perimeter as the prisoners and documents were being loaded, Lieutenant Daniels suddenly spotted an enemy soldier rising from the grass, hand arching back as he prepared to hurl a hand grenade at the chopper. Whiplash's bullets dropped him before he could complete the throw, so the grenade intended for the interior of the helicopter instead landed within a few feet of Lance Corporal Masters and Butcher One. Even as Whiplash drew in a breath to yell, Lieutenant Daniels was in motion; gathering his legs under him, he launched himself into a prodigious leap that landed him squarely on top of the grenade. An image of Rhiannon formed in his mind as the cold, hard lump of the grenade transformed into a flash of heat and pressure and pain, then dissolved as the pain vanished and a wall of darkness washed over his senses.

Eyes widening as the grenade landed a few feet away, Lieutenant Kentworthy hurled himself towards it, but as he was in midair, a flying body interposed itself between him and his intended target, landing just as the grenade went off and leaving Lieutenant Kentworthy falling onto the corpse. For a split-second he lay still as he fought for breath, then he scrambled to his knees and rolled the body over, horror and guilt washing over him as he recognized the torn and blackened features of Lieutenant Carl Daniels. A long moment passed as he tried to process what had just happened, then a hand on his shoulder jerked him back to reality as Sergeant Piper grabbed him and began dragging him to his feet. "Come on, we've got to load those prisoners; move yourself!"

Drawing a gasping breath, Lieutenant Kentworthy shook his head to clear it, grabbing Lieutenant Daniels's body and dragging it aboard the nearest helicopter. Hopping aboard after it, he fired his rifle from the open cargo bay as the rest of the team collapsed back on the choppers and gave the all-clear; debris flying in all directions as the mighty birds clawed for safety in the skies overhead. Slumped on the floor of the helicopter, Lieutenant Kentworthy stared in sick horror at Lieutenant Daniels's body, wondering what was going to happen to his wife; so soon a widow after a bride. Why couldn't you have jumped just that little bit sooner? Why couldn't you be the one they're sending home in a bag, and Carl be the one who gets to go home? He had a wife, for crying out loud!

As he stared at Carl's sightless eyes, determination to atone for what he had done in what ways he could hardened within him.

Two Months Later:

Rhiannon stared out the window at the light dusting of snow that covered the ground. It had been an unusually light snow level this year, with less than a foot since

October, but more was expected over the next few days. Fighting down another stab of worry at the lack of letters over the last two months, she tried to tell herself that Carl was just busy, and couldn't find time to write her. A loud purring sounded from around her ankles as Darryl decided that his afternoon nap was over and it was time for her to pick him up. With a smile, Rhiannon bent over, lifting the big cat from where he paced around her legs, listening to his purrs grow deeper with pleasure as she scratched behind his ears. Glancing back out the window, she was startled to see a car pulling into the driveway, and a man in an Army dress uniform stepping out. For a moment, her heart leaped as she thought it might be Carl, but just as quickly, she dismissed the notion. The man walking up the sidewalk was shorter than Carl, and broader-shouldered. Walking over to the door as he knocked, she opened it, Carl staring disdainfully at this intruder on his domain. "Yes, may I help you?"

The man removed his hat, looking extremely uncomfortable as he balanced it on a box with a letter on top. "Mrs. Daniels? I'm Lieutenant Mark Kentworthy. I believe your husband mentioned me in his letters?"

Nodding, Rhiannon smiled a welcome, stepping back. "Why yes, he did. Come on in!"

Biting his lip, Lieutenant Kentworthy obeyed, following her to the living room where she waved him to an armchair by the fire. "So what brings you around here, Lieutenant?"

Lieutenant Kentworthy took a deep breath. "I can't even begin to tell you how sorry I am to have to say this, Mrs. Daniels, but I'm here on behalf of the War Office. I...I am here to inform you that your husband...your husband is dead. He was Killed In Action in the Central Highlands in October."

As Rhiannon's hand went to her mouth and her eyes

filled with tears, he handed her the box. "These were the effects found on his person at the time of his death."

Opening it with shaking hands, Rhiannon sorted through the items: a wallet, the picture of her, now stained with blood and nicked around the edges; the locket she had given him for Christmas the year before, also stained with blood; the knife, and a few other miscellaneous items. Looking back up at Lieutenant Kentworthy, she asked the one question he had hoped she would not ask. "How did he die?"

Grasping the edges of his hat, Lieutenant Kentworthy drew another deep breath, hating himself for the lie he had no choice but to tell. "Well, we were out on patrol in the Highlands, and Charlie jumped us..."

This book was published by

FIRST TIME
PRESS

10% of all the revenue from this book goes to support mission's work. We hope you enjoyed this author's self-edited work.

First Time Press exists to give promising authors a platform to publish their early works. Since its founding, First Time Press has eagerly sought out and received submissions from authors worldwide looking for a chance to be noticed for their extraordinary work.

Each year, First Time Press receives self-submitted manuscripts from undiscovered authors looking to use their talents to bring God glory. Each work is reviewed and examined by an award-winning team of creators. Five manuscripts are hand-picked each year for their raw excellence (ranging anywhere from sci-fi to biographies). These manuscripts are then edited by the author and published "as is" to showcase the creator's undiscovered talent.

First Time Press looks to encourage and celebrate the achievements of those who have a passion and a calling to write. All publishing expenses are covered, and there is no out of pocket cost for these authors once chosen for publication. 80% of all revenue generated from the sales of First Time Press books is given back to their respective authors. Only 20% is deducted, 10% to cover the cost of operations and 10% donated to mission's work.

Other titles from

First Time
Press

Other Worlds and their stories
By J. Riley Peak

The question regarding whether or not other planets share earth's unique ability to rear life is a question many ask. However, I resign myself to the idea that I must leave such a search alone, for why bother talking about planets when one can speak about worlds?

Hearts at War
By Rob Winblad

Sergeant Rick Newman has shipped to Afghanistan with the Marines. After a mission goes wrong and his fiancee's brother is killed in action, he blames himself for her brother's death and the subsequent dissolution of their relationship. Running from the demons that haunt him, he must find it in his heart to forgive himself, even as she has forgiven him.

The Torch Keepers
By Hosanna Emily

A revolution sweeps across the kingdom of Érkeos. A girl finds her city engulfed in the Liberation's emerald flames. But, when she meets Rekém, she rebels against the King. Now Kadira and Rekém could bring destruction to the entire kingdom.